the FAKE SANTA apology tour

JULIE OLIVIA

author's note

♡

I've been blessed to have many holidays full of joy and cheer, but I know that life is not always candy canes and tinsel. That being said, this book is 98% hot-chocolate-out-your-nose laughs, dreamy holiday nostalgia, and sexy silver-fox men. But also about 2% angst. Not a lot, but be kind to your heart when you read, friends.

Also be advised this is **not** a clean romance. This is a **slow burn romance** with **on-page, open-door** sexual content, so mature readers only.

Now put on your favorite classic holiday album, wear your tackiest Santa sweater, make some hot cocoa, and let me take you on this winter wonderland journey!

Happy Holidays!
xoxo, Julie O.

To my mom who once said that Santa is real if you just believe.

I was eleven and confused because everyone kept telling me otherwise, but I understand the sentiment now.

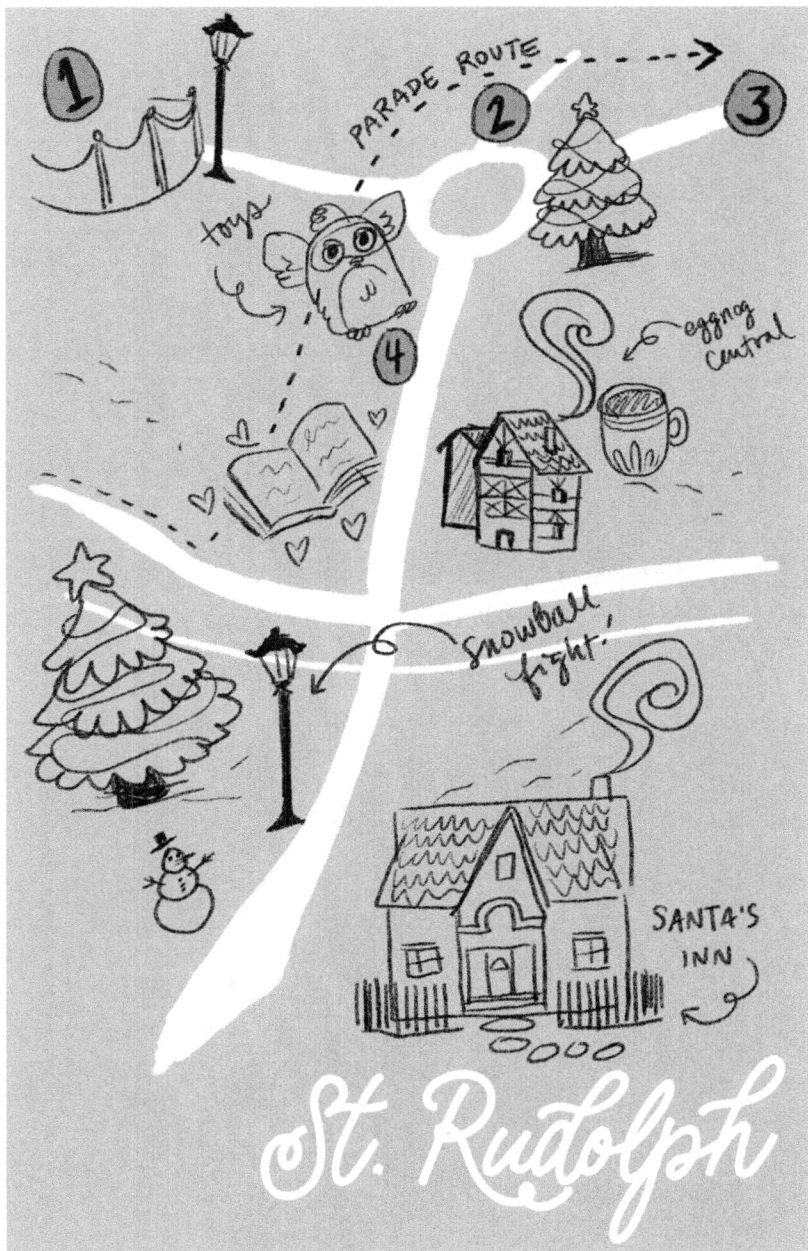

PARADE ROUTE

1

2

3

4

toys

eggnog Central

snowball fight.

SANTA'S INN

St. Rudolph

prologue

1999, TWO DAYS BEFORE CHRISTMAS.

Fake Santa is happy.

Too happy.

But I guess I would be happy too if I could get away with being rude like he and his elves are.

The mall is jam-packed with shoppers. People with puffy coats and pink cheeks, crinkling shopping bags filled with gifts, and boots that crunch from dregs of snow still melting onto the tiled floor. Under the hum of the crowd, I can just barely hear the bells and horns of *Sleigh Ride* over the speakers.

And smack dab in the center, right under the garlands swinging down from the second floor, is a massive, ornamented tree with a throne in front.

The jolly man with the fake white beard is just sitting there.

Smiling.

The silly, dopey man doesn't even know what's coming to him. He doesn't know who I am: Birdie Mae, letter writer and, as my daddy tells me, most determined Girl Scout in the troop.

Now, how to do this…

I look over the layout from a nearby bench. The line to visit Fake Santa is wrapping like a maze around his red and green throne, running up to the bottom of the golden stairs where a giant cutout of a wall-eyed nutcracker is standing. Just under him, inside the toy workshop façade, is a crack in the cardboard.

Right where Santa's pocket is.

Score.

It's sneaking around the stalking elf security guards that'll be the problem. Of course, they're not real elves; they're stooges, just like him. Yeah, a bunch of—

"Whatcha doing?"

I jump at the whispered word and turn to see…another elf.

Well, sort of.

Kind of.

The other elves didn't make my chest feel instantly gooey and weird.

It's his eyes I notice first. Crystal blue with almost a shine to them. And his hair—thick and ginger like my sister's. Not curly like hers though, but straight and almost messy like he runs his hands through it a lot. He looks like he could be in *NSYNC or something.

He's definitely around my sister's age, older and probably in high school, but he's thicker than the boys she hangs around. At least, more than someone like her current gangly boyfriend Brian. In fact, this dude looks more like the football players at Anne's marching band shows. Tall and big.

Yeah, I definitely feel a weird warmth in the pit of my stomach.

"Hello?" he asks with a low chuckle. "You in there, kid?"

"I'm just…watching," I say quickly, trying to puff out my chest. *Confidence.* "Can't I watch?"

He narrows his eyes.

I narrow mine.

"Hang on, didn't Sally just warn you to stay away?" He glances at the yellow-haired elf patrolling near the photo booth area. The same elf who told me 'We don't take letters' and to 'buzz off' in the snottiest tone that I totally wouldn't be able to get away with around Momma.

"No," I respond. "She didn't."

I cross my fingers behind my back, but he doesn't know that.

Sucker.

"Are your fingers crossed?"

"What!" I say much louder than I meant to, so I lower my voice back down. "No."

He laughs, and when he does, it's deep and throaty. My fingers fidget after hearing it.

"Okay, maybe," I admit.

He smiles, and my face feels hot. He's got a dimple, and I've never thought dimples were unsettling, but for some reason it's just not jibing with me. Or maybe it's jibing with me too much.

I shake my head. *Get it together, Beem.*

"I'm just trying to get my letter to the real Santa," I say.

I pull my crumpled envelope out of my pocket and flash it at him. He lifts an eyebrow and glances over to Fake Santa.

"You know this *is* the real Santa," he says in a low voice.

"No, it's not, and you know it."

He squints his eyes. "How old are you?"

"Eleven."

"Aren't you a little too old to…"

"To what?"

He pauses, staring at me for a second before shaking his head. "Nothing. Never mind."

"Well, whatever," I say. "Just…go away."

"Eh, make me."

My mouth gapes open. I mean, I guess I could push him or something, but I've never pushed anyone who wasn't my sister. Plus, that'd get me in loads of trouble, and I'm not going to jeopardize my status on the nice list this close to Christmas. I've already snuck away from Momma for too long, and that may lead to a check mark in the naughty category as it is.

He starts to lean against the column next to us, arms crossed over his stupid-looking green elf uniform, and I know he's not going anywhere. I'm stuck with him. Him and his lean—a lean so casual with a glance off in the distance like a model or something.

It's so captivating that I can't look away.

His eyes twitch over to me, and he smiles. His dimples make my chest pitter-patter a bit faster. If people could have twinkles in their eye like Santa, this guy would have it. And now that I look closer, his eyes aren't fully blue, but more like this weird color that's both gray and blue and really pretty. I didn't know boys could be pretty.

"So what's the game plan here?" he asks.

I'm not getting rid of him, so…

"I'm gonna sneak a letter into his pocket," I say.

"Rad," he says. "Then let's do this."

I shake my head and stick out my chin. "Wait, no, I can do it alone."

He looks off in the distance—that model stare again—then back at me with a boyish smirk.

"And how will you make it past Sally, huh?" he asks,

lifting his chin over in her direction. "She'll totally kick you out this time."

"Whatever," I say. "I won't get caught."

"Okay then," he says. "I mean, it'll be easy-peasy if I help, though."

I look from him to the overwhelming nutcracker setup and then up at the clock.

I don't have enough time to argue. I've been here too long, and Momma is probably already looking for me.

"Fine," I say.

We both sit on the mall floor, me with my legs criss-cross-apple-sauce and him with his long legs outstretched and back still resting against the column. He slid down to sit, and it looked cooler than anything I've ever seen someone do up to this point. Plus, his red Converse have loose laces and Sharpie writing up the side, which Momma would never let us do.

"Alright," he says, leaning in. He smells nice, like Christmas tree pine and peppermint. "If we go around the back on the left…"

"There's the Rudolph stand-up blocking the way. We can't," I say. "But I can crawl through the window cutout."

He shakes his head. "No, that'll draw too much attention. But if we shift Rudolph to the side…" He leans in closer to point out the break in the house's construction.

I gasp. "There's an entrance."

"Atta girl."

My face grows hot. And then my chest. And my hands feel twitchy.

"Um, okay," I say. "Well, let's do this."

"Game time."

He stands then holds out his hand to help me up. I don't take it. This only makes him smile more.

We both sneak around the circular area of the Santa

display. He's tiptoeing like the Grinch, which makes me laugh, but I realize I'm too loud and stop.

"Okay, let's wait here until there's a kid rotation," he says.

I nod, and we both crouch next to the Rudolph standee.

"So what's your letter about?" he finally asks.

"Well," I say, taking it out of my pocket again, "my sister says Santa fired Rudolph, and I'm telling him not to."

"Couldn't Rudolph just get another job?"

"A reindeer with a bright red nose? Yeah, okay," I say, rolling my eyes. "Doubt it."

"What'd you say to him?"

I fumble into the envelope to unfold the letter then clear my throat. "*Dear Santa.*"

"Solid start," he says.

I narrow my eyes. "*Dear Santa.*" I jut out my chin. "*Rudolph had one wish in life—*"

"Good Lord, is he dying?"

I lower the paper.

"Well, it's his last year," I say, irritated he keeps interrupting me. "It'd be horrible if he couldn't fly on his last year."

"I didn't know it was Rudolph's last year."

"Uhhh, what?! It's everyone's last year."

Like duh.

This time he leans his head back to bark out a laugh. It's a beautiful motion. I've never seen such effortless happiness. "I'm sorry?!"

"My sister says the world is ending next year."

"Your sister seems to say a lot of things."

I narrow my eyes. "It's why-two-kay. We're gonna run out of milk and stuff. Don't you watch TV?"

He shrugs. "No, not really."

"We watch *Survivor*," I say. "You don't watch *Survivor*?"

"What's *Survivor*?" he asks. His face is blank, but I think he's messing with me. Anne gets the same expression when she's being a total jerk too.

I scowl. "You'd totally be voted off."

"I guess so," he says, his crooked smile twitching upward again to show one dimple. It's hard to keep frowning, and I hate him for it.

Then his laugh picks up again, and he points at my paper. "Wait, what's that?"

I glance down at my drawings on the letter. *Oh no, is it not obvious?*

"A sleigh," I mumble.

"You drew it for him too?"

"Well, in case an elf gets it first. They can't read, you know."

"Your sister say that?"

"Yes."

He nods slowly. "Right. So, you're illustrating it."

"Duh."

He smiles, and I definitely know he's mocking me now.

"Whatever," I say, folding up the letter and stuffing it back into the envelope. "Let's just get this over with."

"Aw, come on. I'm sorry. No, it's good!" he says.

"Whatever!"

"Well, so, you're not even asking for anything?"

I blink up at him with a scoff.

"*Of course* I've told Santa what I want too," I say. "I've circled the purple Furby no less than three times in the catalogue on Momma's desk. She knows, and she talks to Santa regularly, so I know he knows I know I'm getting a Furby."

He opens his mouth to speak, but then both of us seem

to notice the change at the same time. One kid is leaving Santa's lap sobbing, and the elf standing beside him is walking her off toward the ropes.

There're no more bodyguards.

"Now!" the boy says. "I'll keep watch!"

He shifts Rudolph to the side, giving me room to crawl in.

It's darker than I thought it would be, but I can't let that stop me.

Gotta be brave.

I shuffle over the piles of what feel like cords and cardboard boxes and find a tiny light shining in through the opening to Santa's throne. I crawl over on my hands and knees, twisting to edge out from behind the opening, and right next to my face is my destination.

Santa's pocket.

I reach my hand out, moving my letter closer to the folds in his red jacket. If only I could…

"Hey! Kid!"

Oh no.

I look up. The yellow-haired elf. Sally.

"How did you…" she says, her eyes crazed and wild. Oh god, she's gonna tell my mom.

"I got her," the elf says. But it's not just any elf—it's *my* elf with the ginger hair and the red Converse. "No worries, Sal. I'll take her."

My elf, the boy who was supposed to be keeping watch and definitely *isn't*, now rushes toward me.

"You said—"

"Shh, go go go," he whispers.

I reach into my coat, pull out the envelope, and slip it into Fake Santa's pocket.

Fake Santa shifts in his seat, startled by the commotion

and yelling, but he also seems tired and unconcerned that I just reverse pickpocketed him.

Perfect.

I run off with the elf boy, stumbling in my slippery boots on the tiled floor as he laughs beside me.

"You did it!" he says.

"But you didn't stand guard!" I say, my face hot.

He continues to laugh, clutching his stomach. "I was, but you were right out in the open! What was I supposed to do?"

"You're so mean!"

"Aw, kid, I'm sorry."

He looks like he's trying to stop laughing.

"No, you ruined it."

Then he crosses his arms and lifts a single ginger eyebrow.

"Come on, last I checked he got the letter, right?"

I'm being unfair and I know it, but people are still watching us, and I feel so small.

I kick the ground and mumble, "Yes."

"Then mission accomplished?" He seems wholly unconcerned with who is watching. Maybe it's the confidence of age, but I don't have that.

"Okay, but…how am I supposed to know if he gets it and what if he throws it out and…"

"I'll tell him not to," he says. "Don't worry, kid."

I stuff my hands in my pockets and meet his eyes. He's grinning down at me, and it's kind. He looks like the younger version of Kris Kringle in that animated movie we watch every year.

After a moment, he says, "Wow, you must really love Christmas, huh?"

"Yeah, don't you?"

"Nah."

My eyes practically bulge out of my face.

"What?! Why?"

"I just…" He shifts a little and looks away. "It doesn't matter."

"You're wrong," I say.

He laughs. "I'm *wrong?*"

"Yeah. Christmas is for family and fun and happiness."

His face falls and then he clicks his tongue, shaking his head with it.

"Nah, you'll grow to hate Christmas. Everyone does, I think."

I can feel my face distorting in anger, but I know Momma and Daddy would be mad if I did anything stupid here. Plus, they promised we'd watch holiday specials when we get home, and I definitely don't want that taken away.

"Never," I say. "I'd never hate Christmas. You can't curse me with that."

But at me saying that, he laughs a little then winks. "Can't I?"

My stomach drops. It's cute. And horrible. And wonderful.

I blink once, maybe twice, only as much as it takes to make sure I'm seeing him clearly, because he's got that twinkle in his eye. The dimple. The pinkish nose.

Is he *magic?*

He is.

And he totally just used that magic to curse me.

"Hey, wait, no…"

The intercom clicks on above us and interrupts me.

"Birdie Mae, please report to guest services. Your mother is looking for you. Birdie Mae, please report to mall guest services, thank you."

"Oh no," I groan. "Oh no." I know I'm in trouble now. The intercom means she's been looking for me for a while.

"Birdie Mae? Is that your name?" the elf boy asks with another laugh. "What a name."

I narrow my eyes. "Oh, and what's yours? Something normal?"

He grins. "Name's Nicholas. Nicholas Ryan, but people call me Nic."

I almost gasp, but I hold my breath.

Jolly ol' Saint Nick.

This can't be real.

I gulp. "Well, it was *not* nice to meet you, Nicholas."

"I'd say the opposite, Birdie Mae," he says. "I had a great time. And Merry Christmas."

"No! You *don't* have a merry Christmas."

He gives a small wave and a smile as I slowly walk then hurriedly run away, and I keep picturing that smile all the way to guest services. For once, though, I'm not running in the mall for fear of my momma's wrath, but for fear of losing the memory of Nicholas. Like when you rush to tell someone your dream in hopes that you can remember it for that much longer.

When I get there, Momma is flushed. She always is this close to Christmas.

"Birdie Mae! Thank God. You know not to sneak off like that. Christ."

"...mas," I finish.

She wants to be mad, but instead she grins down at me at the joke. I knew that'd get her.

People tell me all the time that we look the same— mousy brown hair and freckles and all. Someone once asked Momma if she and I were sisters. Anne later told me he was hitting on Momma, which I said was ridiculous because she's married to Daddy.

I want to tell Momma about Nicholas. I'm practically itching to, but I know that'll lead to a talk about being with strangers. I'm already on thin ice, so I curl my lips in and keep it to myself as we walk to the bookstore.

"I can't even imagine how your daddy will make it back home in time with all this traffic…" Momma says as we cross the threshold.

I peek at familiar red curls near the CD aisle. I know they belong to my sister, Anne, because nobody has hair like hers, except Nic maybe. Her curls seem springier than usual, but that's because other hands are running through it.

Oh, EW, Brian's hands!

"Gross!" I yell, scrunching my nose. I look to see Momma's reaction, but she's too distracted by a new Christmas album to have noticed.

"Birdie Mae!" Anne says with a groan.

"Trust me, I'm *not* looking!" I slap my hand to cover my eyes.

"Better not," Anne says, but I can hear the teasing in her voice. "I'll call you later, Brian."

I swear Anne told me just two weeks ago she thought Brian was too gangly and his braces were too big for his tiny mouth. I guess things change when you get braces off.

I wonder if she would have thought Nicholas was cute.

"Brian says Santas here don't take letters," Anne says, tugging my fluffy hood up just to cover my face and annoy me. I slap her hand away. "Did you get him to take yours?"

Maybe I won't tell her about Nicholas after all.

"No," I lie. "I lost it."

"Aw, darn. Sorry, Beem," she says. "Hey Momma, can we get Birdie some more stationary?"

I smile because, okay, sure, sometimes she isn't the worst.

Momma frowns. "Girls, but it's so…"

"Close to Christmas," all three of us say in unison.

Momma purses her lips, looking down at her CD. But Anne is already grabbing a small pack of Christmas cards from the register's line and placing them in Momma's arms.

"Okay, fine," Momma says, waving the pack at me with a conspiratorial wink before the three of us file into line at the register, CD and stationary box in one hand and a swiped candy bar in the other. "We'll get a bar of chocolate for your dad too so he's included. But only one!"

On the ride home, I write under the flash of each streetlight, and I think about Nicholas's words.

'You'll grow to hate Christmas.'

There's no way he's right about that.

Christmas is the best holiday.

How could I ever hate it?

CHAPTER one

Christmas sucks, and traveling during Christmas sucks even harder. Especially when everywhere you turn your own stupid books stare back at you.

I was once told it never gets old seeing your own books in bookstores, but I beg to differ. It was fun the first time. In fact, most things are more exciting the first go-round.

First dates.

First kisses.

First release party.

Everything after that is just a letdown.

And now, as I look at my own backlog of books encircling the built-in display at the airport's shop, I'm not bursting with pride, but am instead haunted by all the Santas I've drawn over the years staring back at me.

My illustrated sexy Santa novels are best sellers. They always have a pink nose, cheeks patted upon with watercolor, and the Birdie Mae signature flop of white hair to make him look younger, more debonaire.

That flop is what makes me the big bucks.

I glance over the titles.

Santa's Big Gift.
Santa's Pink Candy Cane.
Santa's Blue Ornament Balls.

I don't know how I was able to slip that last one past my publisher, but they all laughed, saying how adorable it was.

Adorable. Yes, with a very adorable package in his red trousers.

I roll my eyes at them all. The wiry beards. The raised white eyebrows.

I do love my job, I swear. It's honestly the only thing keeping me together year after year since The Curse of '99. Since…*him.*

But this year? I'm a little done with Santas.

I move on through the airport, sidestepping crowds of people, all wearing simple things like long-sleeved shirts and jeans whereas I'm bundled in not one, but two coats. I'm a Southern bird through and through, but traveling north to write my Santa stories is the only way I can truly capture the holiday spirit. Unfortunately, I can't stand the cold.

My phone buzzes in my coat pocket. I try to fish it out, but my massive mittens are not helping. *Geez, do heaters even exist up here?* I finally rip my glove off with my teeth to fish my phone out and smile before unlocking the home screen.

"I swear you can *smell* my plane landing from two time zones away," I say.

"Beem, you told me you'd call right away," Anne says, exasperated. By the sound of her tone, you'd think she had called me five times before I answered. Unless…I pull my phone away from my ear. *Okay, yeah, she totally did. Total sister move.*

"Give a girl some time to deplane," I say. "Man, this airport is a mess."

I say this right as I'm twirling in a quick circle to avoid the oncoming Tasmanian Devil-like kid with his backpack hitting his bottom in sync with his pounding feet.

"That's what you get for leaving so late in the year," Anne says. "Crowded flights."

"Yeah, well, wasn't exactly my fault I left late."

I mean, it was and it wasn't. It wasn't my fault I got broken up with. It was my fault I wallowed for too long and postponed my annual writing retreat to just five days before Christmas.

There's an awkward silence I do not want to be filled with her questions, so I quickly add, "But I'm fine, Anne! They played *The Santa Clause* as the in-flight movie, so that was nice, and they had gingerbread cookies for the snack. Very festive."

I take the crowded escalator and it slowly lowers me down. The kid in front of me zooms his car along the railing.

"Beem," she starts, and I cringe because *Oh, here it comes.* "Are you sure you're...okay?"

"Anne," I chastise, "no need to get your Christmas lights in a wad. It's fine. I'm fine. Flight was fine," I say, finally letting out a small laugh to ease the tension. "The plane landed in one piece."

"And you?"

"Well, now I'm about to be an icicle. Hang on."

I exit through the sliding glass doors out to the cold. The wind bites at me, and it's not some tender love nip I'm generally quite fine with, but the cut of a knife across your cheeks.

Ah, winter.

I schedule a quick ride share then pull the phone back up to my ear.

"I'm back."

"So, you're an icicle, you say?" she continues. "Does that have to do with the weather or your heart?"

"Very smooth transition, but ouch."

I was hoping the conversation would move on, but no such luck with Anne. In fact, I know what's coming next before she even has to say it. She acts like this is the first time we're broaching this topic, but it's so overdone that I think even Sesame Street's The Count would be impressed.

"It's…just…well, you're going through a breakup." *Fifty! Ah-ha-ha!* "And it's also…that time, you know?"

"My period?" I say deadpan.

"No," she drawls. "The week of Christmas."

I can barely hear her over the wind, the general hum of the people getting into cars, and said cars honking, not to mention the loud holiday music blasting through the outdoor speakers, like it's yelling at me to *feel the spirit*. Even the giant tree in the center of the airport roundabout is flashing bright lights at me.

"Beem?" she asks. *Has she been talking?*

I pull back my sweater sleeve to check the time. Dad's old, gold Omega wristwatch shines back at me. I rub my thumb along the face to clear my previous thumbprint. I'm sure he'd be upset if he saw me doing that, but I'm amazed it even still works. He could get over the fact that it's a little smudgy.

"It's almost midnight your time," I say. "What are you still doing up?"

I bet Anne and Brian are just finishing up a holiday movie with sugar cookies cooling on top of the oven—the pre-cut ones with the little reindeer designs on top. I would normally be there with them, the single aunt in all her lonely goodness, but alas…here I am instead, two time zones in the past.

And then, just barely, I hear the DVD menu theme I know all too well.

"Wait a second, are you guys watching *Elf* without me?"

"Not my fault," Anne singsongs with no shame heard in any syllable. "You left! We've gotta knock some traditions out without you now!"

I was supposed to leave on my annual winter writing trip weeks ago, but that was also the week Stephen decided it was time to break things off.

In a normal year with no heartbreak, I travel to a new place immediately after Thanksgiving dinner. This is when I get the bulk of my brainstorming and writing done for the calendar year. The spring is for illustration work, and the final drafts are in the summer. It's a system I have perfected over six years, and even though I'm getting a late start due to the hazards of dating men who don't want to date me, the schedule still has to happen.

"Do you…do you think you'll have the energy to write your Santa this year?" Anne asks.

The question hits me like twelve angry reindeer knocking into an old woman on Christmas Eve.

"Anne." It's a second warning that she immediately does not heed.

"If it makes you feel better," she says, "I don't think Stephen had nearly as much jolliness as Trevor."

"That's the difference between a mall Santa and a parade Santa."

"Preach."

Okay, let's pause.

There's something you should know.

I have…a *type*.

Listen, it's not a conscious thing. It's not like I go to Santas "R" Us and pick out the perfect white beard and matching squeaky black boots. I can't help that I'm drawn to a certain type of temporary man, and I can't help if that man just so happens to represent something pure and wonderful in December.

It all started with Zack about seven years ago. I met him while taking my nephew to get his last-minute Christmas wishes in at the local holiday arts festival. And there he was: Santa Claus. On the throne with sparkling eyes and cute red cheeks. When we spoke, he was nice and happy—unlike me during the holidays, which is a plus— and, without the fake beard, he was surprisingly young and kinda hot. So when he asked for my number, I got curious and said yes.

In that short December love affair, we went to holiday light shows, took carriage rides with those beautiful clip-clopping horses (yes, they totally clip-clop just like in the songs), and made gingerbread houses from scratch. Little did he know, the tattoos hidden under that red suit of his were going to be the most commitment he'd be getting that year. I broke up with him shortly after Christmas Day. Our personalities ultimately didn't mesh, and it wasn't gonna work.

But the fact remained: I'd never experienced a Christmas season like that since 1999. Not since The Curse. It was fantastical and, best of all, temporary. I was addicted.

So, the following year I dated Randy the mall Santa, another guy surprisingly in his mid-thirties with a decent smile. Under the pillow he used to create his fake Santa gut, there were abs of steel. I was sold. We went to see *The Nutcracker*. We ice-skated. And I broke up with him right after New Year's.

The temporary nature of the second Santa was so appealing. It was amazing that I could make my holidays not suck for once then move on in January like nothing happened. At least, that's my therapist's theory.

So the next year came Mark the stripper Santa. Candy canes. Candy-cane-decorated poles. *His* slightly crooked candy cane, if you get me. Broken up by Christmas Eve.

Then Trevor the parade Santa.

And Frank…who had an authentic white beard and never actually told me his age. It was a low point; don't judge.

Then finally Stephen, the Santa who stayed too long.

Anyone with the right amount of holiday cheer who can call me his ho-ho-ho in bed and has a cute, tight butt that fits into a red suede suit is a man I'm on board with. What can I say? I like the idea of a fantasy man doing fantastical things. It's all a lie in the end, but who cares? All men tell lies, after all. At least these guys are up front about theirs.

Anne asks, almost timidly, "The breakup wasn't *your* decision this time, was it?"

Strike three.

"Anne," I say, my gut clenching tight before I can finish what might have followed my warning tone.

I feel sick, but I'm going to chalk it up to those gingerbread cookies on the plane. Looking back, they seemed stale. I bet I'm just getting slow food poisoning. Much more preferable than *feelings*.

"You know what?" I can hear her clap her hands on the other end of the line like she's readying herself to make a point. "I'll just say it."

"Please don't."

"I'm worried about you this time."

"Why?"

"You dated this dude for *a year*. He went through

almost two holiday seasons! They never last that long. I mean, not that he should have, but…"

I ignore her potential tangent.

"It was nothing," I say.

"He went to Easter."

"It was a fling."

"He moved in with you."

I scoff. "Come on, Anne. You're not Momma—you can't get on my case like this."

"I may as well be."

We both stop, immediately realizing what she said. It's a weird pause, not exactly awkward, but knowing, almost like a solemn moment of silence.

And then Anne says, "You know, Momma's asking about Daddy already…"

The words come slowly because she knows I don't want to hear them. But they still need to be said, I suppose.

I clench my jaw, breathing in slowly. I can't handle it this year. I just can't. Not with the breakup.

And not with the twentieth anniversary of The Curse.

"What did you tell her?" I ask.

"I didn't."

I exhale, seeing my breath puff up in front of me like smoke. God, I wish I smoked. Do people find relief through that? Should I take it up? Is this year the year?

Then Anne asks, "You'll be home in time for Christmas, right Beem?"

I want to say no. I'm home for Christmas every year, opening presents with them in matching pajamas, scarfing down cinnamon rolls and playing with the kids. But this year, this Christmas, and this man…The Curse just got too bad this time.

But I also know I can't let Anne down.

"Yes, I'll be home in time for Christmas," I echo. "Promise."

"You know," Anne says with a laugh, as if trying to lighten this horrific mood I'm now in, "that's what they all say before some big snowstorm or something."

"Don't jinx me," I warn at the same time she laughs again.

My phone buzzes against my ear and I pull it down to see that my ride has arrived and is parked all the way down the lot.

I sigh. "Oh Christ."

"...mas?" she finishes.

"Nice."

"Enjoy your retreat and just leave by Christmas Eve, alright? I'll have cookies ready in the oven for you, squishy just how you like them. And..." *Here we go.* "Don't let him ruin Christmas for you, Beem."

I don't know if she means fake Santas of breakups past or the thought of our dad, to be honest.

"I would never" is all I say, because he couldn't ruin Christmas—neither Stephen nor my dad.

Dear Saint Nicholas Ryan already did that for me by cursing me with bad Christmases forever.

CHAPTER Two

THIS YEAR'S DESTINATION WAS RECOMMENDED BY MY editor, Erica. She said this small town was so magical it made her believe in miracles again. If you ask me, I think that's because she and her husband experimented with some kinky new ideas and just so happened to conceive their third child that weekend, but that's beside the point.

A good forty minutes from the airport, the small town of St. Rudolph is a Thomas Kinkade holiday card personified. Each building is white with crisscrossed dark plank motifs and some form of garland along the windows. Every rooftop is lightly dusted with evidence of past snowfall. Though, when I look out the window, I don't see any snow currently falling, so that's good.

We drive through the downtown area for only half a mile before we reach my destination. There's a bookstore, a pub, and even a mom-and-pop toy store. Streetlamps light up the town, but even if they weren't there, not one single house is missing strings of Christmas lights. Those puppies could illuminate the roads all on their own.

People stroll on the sidewalks in heavy coats and beanies, carrying shopping bags. Somehow, with the exception of maybe one child recovering from getting hit by a snowball and crying, every person seems to be in excellent spirits. A perfect place to get into my warped headspace to write about discreetly naughty Santas.

Though, seriously, somebody should check if that child is okay...

My ride stops in the middle of the street to drop me off in front of a two-story house with a wooden sign out front swinging by two small chains.

Santa's Inn.

I couldn't have dreamed of a better place if I tried. I'll have to thank Erica later with candy canes and maybe a vibrator for her and her husband.

After checking in with a sweet older lady named Dorothy who looks like she's one more wrinkle away from reindeer running her down, I'm finally plopping down on the twin bed in my room. I can still hear the chatter of voices outside, the distant crackle of the fireplace in the common area downstairs, and the creaking of the floorboards as other residents settle in for the night.

It's delightful.

And yet...my thoughts drift from the holly-jolly-happy ones I should be having and instead over to Stephen, who's likely now packing up his stuff in my living room back home.

He hasn't even texted me.

No. No, it doesn't matter.

We're over it. Finite. He broke up with me.

I should have known he was a mistake from the start. Santa Claus is only here for the holidays, and so should fake Santas be as well. That's the whole point. But Stephen overstayed by nearly a *year.* He was the first Santa who made me genuinely laugh. He was also the first Santa who ended it before I could.

I close my eyes, inhaling deeply.

Don't let him ruin Christmas.

I'm here to write happy books, and that's what I'll be

doing. But I need to get in the proper holiday spirit or else I'll be coming up with ideas to the tune of *Blue Christmas*, and if I do that one more year, Erica and my publisher may disown me forever.

So, I get out of bed and trail out the door. No better way to get into the spirit than with some good ol' spiked eggnog. There was that cute pub I passed on the way in, and I bet it's even cuter when I'm blasted out of my mind on liquid sugar.

Already bundled in my two coats, I head out, instantly tucking my gloved hands back into my pockets for protection. In the small amount of time I've been inside, it's already started to snow.

Crap.

I swear if Anne actually jinxed me…

No, happy thoughts. Christmas thoughts. Pretending to be in a Hallmark movie thoughts.

It's a ten-minute walk to the pub with the wreath on the door. It's an endearing old building with a creaky door that reveals a cramped main room with colorful string lights all along the perimeter walls and the bar. There are patrons scattered in groups of two or three at wooden high-tops, and the low hum of chatter and laughter is enough to lift my spirits even marginally.

I glance at Dad's wristwatch, rubbing along the face again. It's nearing midnight. I don't know when this place closes and I don't want to be *that person* who orders right before, but also nobody else seems eager to leave so I grab a seat at the bar anyway.

I twist my body away from the countertop, slinging my purse over my head and trying to place it on the back of my chair.

I hear the bartender already asking if I want anything. His voice is deep like the hollows of my empty stomach—

geez, those gingerbread plane cookies did nothing—but the tone also has some type of light spring to the end of each syllable. Optimistic like everything else in this town. Warm and comfortable like heated cinnamon.

"You got any eggnog in this North Pole?" I ask absentmindedly—*ah!*—finally finding the hook to hang the strap of my purse.

Then, the bartender answers, but the tone is now husky. Not cinnamon—just deep horchata spice.

"Is that a joke, ma'am?"

My hair stands on end.

"What?" I twist around, but then just as fast as I move, I'm suddenly also choking on my words. Literally sputtering through spit that definitely went down the wrong pipe.

I would say *a* man is my bartender, but no…I'd be wrong. It's *him*.

Again.

Santa Claus. But…he's *insanely hot?*

This must be some type of cruel joke by the universe.

My previous Santas were handsome, but even they didn't look like this. Not this hot-bartender Santa with massive biceps that look like he slings a burlap sack over his shoulder every day of every month instead of the fabled once a year. This man with ridges of abs I can partially peek at through his tight white tee.

And his hair. Wow, this guy's hair looks like he could be the poster child for shampoo commercials. He's the picture of glorious health with the sides trimmed close and clean and thick, silver-fox locks up top. It's gelled over a bit, but with it being after midnight and likely a long shift if I had to guess, he's got one or two pieces flopping down on his forehead. It's hot. It's effortless. And he's freakin' bearded.

He's a hot younger Santa.

Ho ho *oh freaking no*.

He's staring at me. At my brown, messy airplane hair. At my stupid freckles. I have definitely looked better.

"Sorry," he says with a small shake of his head, his hard lines fading to a gentler expression. I don't know which I prefer more: the face that is kind and sweet with more rounded features that say, 'What do you want for Christmas, little girl?' or the other with straight, harsh lines that make me wanna say, 'You, Daddy.'

But I digress.

"No, don't be," I say, waving my hand. "I…wait, what are you apologizing for?"

He scoffs in a half gesture of a chuckle. And *oh my Santa* it's deep and throaty and…

"I'm a bit sensitive about the whole Santa thing," he says.

"I don't think I…"

"The North Pole comment," he says, laughing with deep dimples and lines tugging at the edges of his eyes. It's handsome. Can a laugh be handsome? "I get compared to Santa a lot." *Do you, now?!* He shakes his head with a smile. "Uh, bit of a sore subject for me, I guess."

I don't say what I'm thinking: that he's a super-hot Santa and the comparison is totally reasonable. I instead say the second-best thing, which is, "I don't see the resemblance."

So, never mind, that was the *worst thing* I could have said.

One of his thick, graying eyebrows rises in response, a slight tug at the pink lips under that beard of his.

Well, I can't pull back now.

"Nope," I say, popping the P. "Not one bit."

"Not with the gray beard?"

"No, you know, it's…more…George Clooney."

WOW. Way to call him hot, you freak.

"George Clooney," he echoes.

"George…ahem…Clooney."

"Right."

It's awkward. I've made it awkward.

"Well, maybe," I say, in an effort to make it *un*awkward, "a little like Santa too. It's the twinkle in your eye."

"Ah, the twinkle?"

A twinkle I've only ever seen in one person before: the Cursebringer, Nicholas Ryan. Which means this guy is gonna be no good; I just know it. But, with each second, his smile grows wider. And I sink just a little bit lower into my seat because my heart is pounding and did I mention he's *hot?*

He doesn't say anything. I can tell he's making me suffer and drown in my own weirdness. So, naturally, I keep talking myself deeper into a hole.

"Yeah," I say. "Your eye twinkle…it's…nice."

He narrows his eyes with a sneaking smile pulling at his lips, and I throw my hands up in surrender.

"I meant," I start, "like, a holiday bartender type of nice. Definitely not Santa. Definitely not."

The man chuckles and it seems genuine, like my torment is his night's entertainment. I want to think, *What a jerk*, but the laugh is low and lovely and rough. Manly. A lumberjack Santa.

Why am I like this?!

"Eggnog, you said?" he asks.

I nod.

Mr. Not-Santa turns to go to the mini fridge behind him. He bends over and, holy smokes, that *ass*. I didn't even know they made jeans like that. So perfectly fitted. So rugged. I also didn't know a man could have a larger donk than my own, but he's somehow achieved that too. It's round and seems toned and hard. I wonder if it would be if I poked it.

I snap out of my thoughts when he places my tumbler down on the bar top with a loud *thunk*. When did he mix it? When did it get placed on a tiny, cute, snowflake-adorned napkin?

He quirks an eyebrow at me.

I curl my lips in.

I can't talk to him any more. If I do, I know where the conversation will lead. I'll find myself with another Santa in my bed. He doesn't know it yet and I'm not even sure how I'd finagle it, but I, Birdie Mae, always take Santas to bed. It's a gift and a curse.

But not this time. No sir.

No more Santas.

"Out-of-towner, right?" he asks.

But darn, if he wants to talk, who am I not to respond?

I'm a woman with manners. Definitely not a woman with a problem.

"Did the eggnog give it away?"

He lifts his chin at me. "The double coat."

I look down at myself.

"What? I'm cold. It's snowing."

"The pink cheeks."

"Yours are pink too." I laugh. "Weirdly a lot like someone else we both know too, but I won't talk about it. You know, since it makes you uncomfortable."

Why are you flirting? Stop it. Stop it now.

His eyebrows rise. He sucks his teeth and leans forward on the countertop. The shoulders under his tee flex. I want to touch them.

"Well, aren't you full of fun and games," he says.

Oh my god. Is he flirting? He's flirting.

I finally take a sip of my drink. A victorious one.

And then I absolutely spoil it.

"All the reindeer let me play."

He scrunches his eyebrows together, and I shake my head.

"I mean...it was...a Rudolph reference. I..."

"I get it," he says with a curl of his lip.

"Ofcourseyoudothat'sdumb," I mumble, knocking back another large gulp of my eggnog and slamming it onto the counter.

He chuckles again, shaking his head. "Not a lot of people order eggnog."

"You're saying you know everyone's order?"

"Most."

"Do you know every person here too?"

"Yes."

"Confident. Okay, who is that?" I jerk my head toward a random man at the opposite end of the bar.

"Tim," Mr. Not-Santa answers immediately, leaning in to whisper the next bit of information. He smells nice, like winter. "Has five cats and all of them are named Fluffy."

"Come on."

He holds his hands up. "I'm serious. Can't make that up."

Down the bar someone yells a quick "Hey!" at Not-Santa, who places his hand down, knocking on the wood like he's announcing his exit. "I gotta go help them, but I'll be back, you."

Be back?

No. No, I can't.

"Oh, no, wait, I'm just heading out," I say. "Can't stay. Hate Christmas, you know." I point up to the ceiling as if indicating the holiday music playing over the speakers.

Saying I hate Christmas is not entirely a lie. The Curse

makes Christmases difficult, regardless of how much I *want* to enjoy it.

He pauses mid-step, pursing his lips, forcing little whiskers of his gorgeous, well-trimmed beard to poke out like cute porcupine needles. "Sure you do. I'll be back."

Well, dang it. And it's not like I can leave. I gotta pay and tip, and I don't have cash.

I watch him at the other end of the bar, serving water to the man supposedly named Tim. In about five seconds, the hot Not-Santa bartender is back.

"So, why do you hate Christmas?" he asks me. "You came to the most Christmassy town in the U.S."

"Bad things happen near Christmas," I say, spouting it out as fact which it is. To me, at least. He opens his mouth to respond, but I continue quickly. "And you? Do you hate Christmas?"

"No, I love it," he says.

"Really?"

"Yep, but, here's a juicy secret..." He leans in. I long to be in on some super secret with him, so I match the movement. He whispers, "I hate the Santas."

"For shame. But go on." I sip my drink with a smile as he balances elbows on the counter with an equal smile.

"I *loathe* them," he says. And the word is serious. Hard lines on his face.

It's so hot.

"Oh," I say.

"Scourge on society. Except for Tim down there. He's cool."

"He's a Santa?"

"Best one, if you ask me."

This dude clearly hasn't seen himself and how similar he looks to the man in the red suit. I'd put him at a solid first place.

"And you…you love Santas or something?" he asks. "I should feel ashamed, you said?"

I gulp. Well, if love is synonymous with bedfellows gone wrong, sure. But he doesn't need to know that.

"It's…complicated," I say.

"If it makes you feel better, I used to like Santas and hate Christmas. Somewhere along the way they got switched."

"Doesn't make much sense."

"Nah, not really."

He smiles, and I see those dimples poking out from under his beard.

Oh boy.

And then there's a crash of glass and Tim over in the corner is suddenly down.

"Ohmygod," I say, practically falling out of my bar stool to run over and help the guy.

But hot-bartender Not-Santa is already there before me, crouching beside him with one hand at his back and the other clutching his hand to help him up.

"Alright there, Tim?" he asks.

"Heyyy there, Mr. Claussss," Tim slurs. "I thin' it's gettin' late."

I cringe, but Not-Santa bartender is all smiles, using those strong biceps of his to lift Tim up in an effortless motion.

"I know, pal," he responds. "And I thought I cut you off hours ago. What's up?"

The man fumbles in his pocket, pulling out a flask with a sheepish smile.

Not-Santa smiles. It's half-hearted.

"Let me call Susan, alright?" he says, pulling out his cell from his blue jeans and dialing.

I hold my hands out to steady a swaying Tim, who is

sort of staring at me.

"You okay?" I ask him directly.

"Susan'll get me." It's slurred. I scrunch my nose at the scent of booze on his breath, but then Tim smiles at me and it's one of those cute old man smiles with squinty eyes and big cheeks that is weirdly hard not to smile back at.

Not-Santa stands, bringing the phone to his ear and muttering, "Hi Sue. We've...oh, already on your way?" Followed by a bark of a laugh. "Dang, like clockwork. Okay, sounds good. I'll bring him out front for ya."

Not-Santa hangs up, tugging at the knees of his pants before bending down to Tim's and my eye level.

"Susan is on her way. Let's get you outside, alright?"

I hold out my arm for Tim. "I'll help."

Not-Santa looks at me, a slow smile easing across his features as he nods. "Alright then."

We lift Tim up, his arms spread over both our shoulders, our height differences making our walk to the front door decidedly lopsided. When we make it outside, there's already a car there with a woman rolling down her window. She doesn't look old enough to be his wife, so I'm assuming she's his daughter.

"Not too bad of a night, I hope?" she asks us.

I open the door, and Not-Santa shuffles sideways to lower Tim in.

"Nah, he's fine." he says. "Snuck in some, though."

She sighs and shakes her head, but no real response is given.

"I'll talk to him... Tell the family I said hi," Not-Santa says.

"Always will. Cooper says he wants a rematch with that snowball fight, you know."

"Tell him any time."

She tucks her chin in. "I'd watch your back then."

They both laugh and then Tim is driven off like a wish in the night.

Not-Santa looks to me and pats his thighs as if to say 'Well that's that' then turns to go back in. Stupidly, I follow, taking the same bar stool in front of him.

I don't know what just happened, but I think I'm a bit too committed now to leave, so I sip my eggnog and watch him in silence. The muscled arms, the thick muscled thighs that fill out those jeans of his, the Timberland boots underneath...

Am I drooling? I can't be. I shouldn't be.

I instead sip my one drink.

People start to leave after a bit. They're getting up and trekking out into the snow, which I can hear whirling past every time the door opens and closes behind them.

But I'm staying. With hot Not-Santa.

Anne will be so mad at me.

I hear a huff of air and find him in front of me again, all smiles with a slight tilt to his head.

"Still here," I say, raising my hand like a dork.

He chuckles.

Ugh, god it's perfect.

"Listen, I've got to close up," he says. "But...you're free to stay if you want. I'll even make you another eggnog on the house."

"You buttering me up?"

"If it's working..."

He lifts a single eyebrow, and my heart rate speeds up.

Should I? What would this lead to? Well, I think I know...but, is it a good decision? He'd be a temporary fling, which has *my type* written all over it. And it's a small town I'll never revisit. And he's got those dimples.

So maybe...maybe I could.

"You're sure?" I ask.

He shrugs and laughs in a way that seems more to himself than to me.

"Don't take this the wrong way, but you seem sad," he says. Wow, that got poured over me like a bucket of ice water. Definitely not where I thought it was going. I open my mouth to retort, but he continues. "Or confused. Or both, I don't know. It's like watching a kicked puppy, and I can't just push you out in the snow, can I?"

I frown.

"I'm not the kicked puppy," I say. "You are with your… your…" I can't think of anything because he's been so cheery up to now.

"Right," he says, smiling. "You're *definitely* sadder."

"Nuh-huh."

"Yeah-huh."

"Okay, listen, maybe I am a bit sad," I say. "And that's fine, okay? But I don't want your pity. I'm just here to get into the holiday spirit and get some work done." I hold up my drink. "Eggnog drinks help."

His grin is slow and sweet, popping those dang dimples in with it.

"Fine. No pity from me." He wipes a rag over the countertop, forcing me to pick up my drink. I raise an eyebrow. He raises one in return. "But no bugging me while I work, okay? I wanna get home."

"Gotta feed the reindeer, right?"

He stops, twisting in place and biting his cheek. I wonder if he's angry at my last stab at flirtation, wonder if I crossed a line. But, no, I see the glimpse of a smile through his neatly trimmed gray beard.

"You're joking about Santa again?" he asks.

"Oh, no, reindeer are no joke," I say, straightening my spine.

He smiles, looking off as if to say, 'This woman.' "Then yes, one in particular is a bit sick."

Oh, he's playing along now.

I smile back. "Red nose, right?"

"How'd you guess?"

"Just a hunch."

He sighs, leaning forward on the bar top. I can see his muscles flex with the motion. It's tantalizing and I can't look away. I don't even try to hide it.

"You know," he says, "I'm serious about all that Santa stuff. Comparisons aren't my favorite. Even if they are flirty."

Flirty.

"Then why the beard?" I ask. "It's so very Santa."

"Have you tried living up north without one?"

"Then why are you also smiling?"

"Because a cute out-of-towner with freckles is flirting with me in my bar." He leans in, voice deep and throaty once more. "And I'm a sucker for it. And maybe I wanna see you just a bit longer."

Oh holy night…

I try not to let my nerves show, but my foot is shaking a little underneath the bar.

Play it cool.

I mock-gasp. "What will Mrs. Claus think?"

He barks out a laugh. "You're so…" His hands slap his thighs before pointing an accusatory finger at me. "Nope. No. I take it back." He steadies both hands on the lip of the bar. "You absolutely cannot stay."

I laugh. "No, wait!" I reach out my hand, letting it land on top of his. In comparison, his hands look like bear paws. And my heart is now racing because of how rough and warm they are.

His eyes glance from my hand up to my face. He

tongues his cheek. "Fine. But you have to promise one thing."

"What's that?"

He twists his palm to reposition us so my hand is now in his. Nerves zip down my chest across my stomach and between my thighs.

"Promise me…that you will detest Santas from this day forward. Loathe them. To your absolute core."

I laugh. "What?"

"Join the Hate Santa club. Seriously, we have better cookies that we don't give him."

"Cute."

"Yeah, well…" His voice fades off as he smiles at me.

Okay, I'm more messed up than I thought. Truly. I have a younger-looking Santa in front of me telling me to hate all others, and I can feel my nerves jolting at the thought.

I can't do another Santa. I can't. I shouldn't. But him…he's temporary. A fling in a town I will never revisit. And that's the whole point of a holiday hookup, right? He's the ultimate Christmas miracle after my bad breakup.

He quirks one eyebrow.

Okay, just one more temporary holiday fling. Just one more then I promise I'm done, universe.

"Whatever you want," I say, my voice a low whisper.

His eyebrows jump up then back down.

"Good. I'll take it."

CHAPTER *three*

I HELP MR. NOT-SANTA CLOSE THE BAR BY MOPPING THE floors. I try to bend this way and that to accentuate my sexiness, but when I've got a wet mop and two coats on, I'm not sure how effective it truly is. When he locks the front door, jiggling the handle for security, then looks me up and down, I know it doesn't matter.

"Where are you staying?" he asks.

Oh yes. He's absolutely coming home with me.

I turn to start walking, and he follows.

Our stroll is mostly quiet. It's well past two in the morning and there's just the crunch of snow beneath our feet. I can sense him, feel the warmth of him even if it's just in my head. The wind blows toward me, sending over a familiar smell, the scent of pine with a sprinkle of peppermint.

It's the second time I've smelled...*him* tonight. The Cursebringer. Nicholas Ryan. And it still bugs me. Like this is some portion of The Curse peeking through.

"So, what's your weird thing with Santas?" I ask, breaking our silence and my own spiraling thoughts.

He chuckles. "It's a secret."

"Ooh, I like secrets."

He grins, rolling his eyes. "I'll tell you about my Santa hate if you tell me why you love them so much."

Oh yes, let me totally explain that I only like dating Santas and you're the hottest one so far and that a Santa just broke up with me and, oh, have we mentioned that you look like a Santa too?

"Yeah, no thanks," I say.

"Aw come on," he says. "You tell me yours, I'll tell you mine."

"Nope."

"Well then…" He lifts his chin. "You won't know my weird thing after all."

"Mysterious."

"I like to think it adds to my appeal."

I smile, and something in me feels bold. I mean, he's walking me home anyway, isn't he?

"It does," I answer. "I want to see what else is so appealing too."

His hand goes to my lower back. My heart soars and my face grows hot. I notice he doesn't wear gloves, which makes it so I can feel each individual finger as they move up and down my spine. Every motion is so sensual and heated.

The inn I'm staying at is up ahead, so I stop in place, glancing down at my dad's watch then back up at him.

"That's me."

"Ah."

"And…would you like to…" I throw my thumb over my shoulder at the inn.

"Dorothy doesn't like it when guests bring people back," he says.

So it is on his mind. This is happening. This is totally happening.

"Dorothy?" I ask.

"The owner."

I was so distracted by him that I forgot I met her.

I lean against the white picket fence enclosing the inn's yard. "Do you know everyone?"

He nods. "I've been here a while."

"Long enough to know how to avoid Dorothy, maybe?" I ask.

He lowers his gaze, looking up at me with heavy-lidded eyes and thick, beautiful eyelashes.

"Maybe."

I walk backward as he takes steps forward, both of us dancing some odd tango toward the front door of the inn. We're not saying what is happening, but we're not exactly walking away either.

It feels like I'm at prom and he just walked me home. There's that buzz of electricity before the end-of-night kiss or the other…planned stuff. It's the anxiety of needing to be quiet so as not to wake the parents—or, in this case, the innkeeper.

We waltz across the cobblestones to the covered front porch stoop where we both stop. But then my eyes dart up and I spot a pesky little thing: mistletoe hanging from the porch ceiling.

The universe loves me. It cares for me. It's totally giving me the green light to sleep with this Santa.

"Should we really go in the front door if Dorothy is that strict?" I ask.

He grins. "Why? Do you want me to sneak in through your window instead? Maybe even the chimney?"

"Sounds unsafe," I say. "And like we'd get in trouble."

He tilts his head to the side, and I see it again in his crystal blue eyes: that twinkle. A genuine kind of thing.

"Do you avoid trouble?" he asks. Then he leans in, hands placed in his pockets, and his next words heat the shell of my ear as he whispers, "Or are you more of a bad girl?"

I, feeling on top of the world and high on him, say back, "I'm whatever you want me to be."

He gives a low grumble in his throat, and I am gone from this world. Absolutely keeled over. Dead-zo. I don't think there's ever been something hotter than that before.

But it's absolutely cut off by that same, familiar scent that haunts my dreams: pine, peppermint.

Why can't the Cursebringer leave me alone? Why is he haunting me with this person with the same scent, the same dimples, even the same eyebrow lift and...

Wait.

No.

It would be insane, but...then again...

"We haven't exchanged names yet, have we?" I ask.

"Have we not?" he says, taken aback by the shift in my tone.

"We haven't," I say.

"Fine then, but I'll lose my mysterious small-town bartender thing."

"I can deal."

He chuckles and extends his hand out to me. "I'm Nicholas. People just call me Nic, though."

And my heart stops.

The dreaded name. The cursed name. My epic movie villain.

No. There's absolutely no way this is *my* Nicholas. It couldn't be possible. He was a cute ginger back then. But that was twenty years ago. People age, and...did my Nicholas age this well? Did he go gray prematurely? It would seem unfair for my villain to look so good, but...yes, in the light of the inn's twinkling lights, there's some ginger remaining in that graying beard of his.

But, no, it can't be.

"Did you always live here?" I ask. The skepticism is oozing from my tone, but I don't care.

This is make or break.

Please say you've always lived here. Please please please.

"Caught me," he says with a smile. "No, I was born and raised in Georgia. I didn't think I had an accent, but…" I'm cringing. I can feel the cold against my teeth. I can't control my facial expressions almost as much as I can't control how much the universe absolutely hates my guts.

It's him. Nicholas Ryan. Cursebringer of '99.

"Balls," I whisper.

He narrows his eyes. "What was that?"

"Mother-effing Christmas balls."

"Do we…know each other?"

My stomach is imploding. I need a cold rag on my forehead. A bathroom, even.

I double over, supporting my weight on my knees. "Oh God. I've got to go."

He reaches out for my elbow. "Wait, what did I say?"

"I can't. Sorry. I just…I can't."

I pull back, and he lets me go. I punch in the key code on the inn door and shimmy through when it unlocks. I just barely see his gorgeous face disappear when I shut it.

I slide down the door and onto the crocheted welcome rug.

I can't believe I've entered my personal nightmare.

I can't believe he's here.

Twenty years later.

So many bad Christmases.

And he continues to haunt me.

First in spirit and now in the flesh.

I'm leaving first thing tomorrow.

It's official. The universe is teaching me a lesson. I should have known.

No more Santas.

And definitely no Nicholas.

I go to my room, set my holiday alarm, then turn over and fall asleep in my airport clothes, listening to the taunting sound of jingle bells ringing outside.

CHAPTER *four*

FOUR DAYS BEFORE CHRISTMAS

I saw Mommy kissing Santa Claus, underneath the mistletoe—

My hand hits the alarm harder than I intended. In fact, the morning yields lots of unintendeds.

I should have known the moment I woke up that my dreams were omens. I dreamt of Santas with nipple piercings yelling at me that Rudolph losing his job was my fault.

Not good.

And now, I feel the cold biting at my ankles like some angry puppy.

It's freezing.

Another not-good thing.

And my chattering teeth won't shut up.

Ugh, I'm crawling out of my skin.

I roll over, peeking out two fingers to split open the blinds. The roads are coated in snow like some horrible holiday avalanche. Even the cars that were parked on the street last night are now just lumpy hills.

No no no.

I quickly jolt out to grab my phone—OHMYGOD THE COLD—then throw the covers over my head to form a heat hut.

I bypass the weather app to swipe open the only one that truly matters: airlines. I look for flights out of here. Out of St. Rudolph. Away from the cold and Nicholas.

Nicholas.

Christ, how did he get back into my life?

How did this happen? Why does the universe hate me?

No. Okay, flights—let's go.

Except…there are no flights.

Nothing.

I scroll, refreshing the page over and over.

Nothing. Not in or out. At least, not at an airport than isn't almost three hours away.

I put my phone back on the dresser just in time for the screen to light up and have my sister's face beaming back at me. It's a photo of her decked out in her Southern fall family photoshoot best—tights and infinity scarf in all their glory.

I grab it, curling my arm back under the blankets like a party blower coiling in.

"Birdie Mae!" she says in a panic when I answer. "I just saw the forecast." *Of course she checked.*

"It's horrible," I mumble.

"The snow can't possibly last past a couple days, right?"

"Stop jinxing me!" I groan, running a hand down my face. But my fingers are too cold to leave the safety of the quilt, so I tuck them back between my legs for the warm thigh oven.

I mutter, "Son of a Kringle. It's cold."

"Don't panic," she says.

"I'm not panicking," I whisper-hiss. "*You're* panicking."

"Well, Beem, you might miss Christmas."

And at those words, there's a tinge of…relief? What if I stayed here for Christmas? I wouldn't have to face the realities of Christmas at home tainted by The Curse.

But, no, Nicholas is here.

It's like I have two devils on my shoulder.

What the heck happened to the angel?

"Okay, less freaking out and better news," Anne says. "How was last night? Is the town cute?"

No. Because it has *him*, the curse of Christmas past that walked me right to my front door. I could have invited him in like the holiday-cheer-sucking vampire that he is, but I didn't.

At least I did one thing right.

"It is nice, right?" Anne asks after I don't respond.

"It's a lot of feet of snow," I say, peering through the blinds again. "Like, a ton. Like, an army of feet."

"Ew, stop talking about feet."

"Sorry."

"Well, look at the bright side—you can get some writing done!" she says with far too much cheer. It must be the sugar cookies spiking her blood sugar or something. "You can explore the town. Get to see some folks in the happy holiday snow! Soak up that Christmas cheer."

Anne is rambling. She does that when she's nervous. What's she not telling me is that she's scared she'll be alone with Momma on Christmas. We've never been apart on Christmas Day. Not since '99. Not since *that* day.

"Yeah, I'll go explore I guess," I say, curling under the covers to heat my ears.

"As long as you're here for Christmas Day…for Momma."

I exhale, letting the warm air fill the blanket fort and

trying to keep my thoughts to dancing sugar plum fairies instead.

———

I lie there for a while imagining my book idea instead of actually writing. I tell myself it's a productive use of time (it's not, but the only ideas I have are Santas dressed in all black here to ruin Christmas. A sexy Krampus. A Christmas with a babysitter and the killer is inside the house...)

A bartending Santa?

No, not Nicholas.

I need inspiration. Maybe Anne was right—walking around is what I need, and if I happen to see Nicholas? I'll just punch him. No, I wouldn't. And who's to say I'd even run into him? It's a small town, but it's not *that* small, is it?

Eventually I decide to bite the bullet and go. I bundle up in a scarf and beanie and coat number one followed by coat number two then trudge down the creaky stairs and out the door.

The outside immediately sucks.

The sidewalk is crunchy, and my feet feel instantly frostbitten. Even with my scarf pulled up so only my eyes are visible through all my layers, I'm cold. I'm convinced my eyeballs are freezing out of my head.

I need warmth.

When I finally reach the edge of downtown, I lumber into the first store on the corner: the cute bookshop. My teeth chatter louder than the jingling bell above the door, but it's warm and that's all that matters. My scarf is wrapped so tight and it's now so stuffy I'm practically choking.

And then suddenly I am. Sort of—at least on my anxiety, because there *I* am.

My sexy illustrated Santas adorn an array of books along the countertop. Tight clothing and mildly seductive eyes. All with my signature swoop at the bottom and my byline.

I can't do this right now, so I refocus and follow the source of warmth. I shuffle and stumble through the stacks, following the heat like a bloodhound until I get to the bottom of a stairwell. At the top there's a door propped open.

I practically hobble up the stairs until I'm peering through the open door.

A fireplace next to a reading nook is nestled on the other side.

Yes yes yes yes.

I rush over, hopping onto the soft leather couch. I *sink* into it.

Ah, it's the good kind of worn leather, slightly cracked but practically begging for a butt.

It's nice for about two seconds until I suddenly smell fresh pine and peppermint followed by a gruff voice that says, "Well, if you wanted to tell me you were interested, you could have just called."

Twisting in place, I look behind me, and—wham bam thank you ma'am—there he is.

Mother-jingle-belling *Nicholas*.

"Okay, so you're also a stalker," I say. "Great. Good to know."

He barks out a laugh. "I'm sorry, *who* is the stalker here?"

Of course he thinks I'm the one in the wrong, but last I checked, I'm the one sitting here with my back turned when he popped up randomly.

"It's a public bookstore," I bite out.

"Right. With an apartment above it."

Hold up, what?

"…what?" I slowly mumble.

He gestures around the area, specifically the bed.

Oh. A bed. How did I miss that?

I blink a few times, taking in the pots and pans hanging from the ceiling over a kitchenette in the far corner, the array of fancy liquor bottles displayed on a shelf, a couple guitars hung on the wall, and the small pile of neatly arranged dumbbell weights.

Yes, I suppose most bookstores do not have a tiny home gym, do they?

"I live above the bookstore," he says. "Welcome to my home. I guess."

"Why was the door open?" I ask quickly.

"Everyone in town knows I live here," he says. "So nobody really comes up. I just don't think about it, I guess."

"Why would…how…I'm sorry…I…"

I can't form the words I need fast enough, so instead I opt not to.

I stand, grab my gloves, and stumble out and down the stairs with no more words. I don't owe him anything except maybe an apology for barging into his apartment, but he barged into my life twenty years ago to place The Curse, so I guess now we're even.

When I get to the front door and open it, I instantly pause. I may not be ready for Nicholas, but the bite of the wind whipping through the door is another obstacle I can't endure. When I turn to go back into the store, he's there. All of him in a cute brown, corded sweater. His thick biceps stretch the material as he crosses his arms over his chest. He's a glorious picture of a man.

THE FAKE SANTA APOLOGY TOUR

"I'm trapped," I blurt out.

"What?" he asks with a laugh. Another beautiful chuckle from that throat of his that bobs with each movement like he's entertained by the world around him. "No, you're not. But you are making me nervous with all that shivering." Nicholas reaches around me and lifts one eyebrow. "May I shut the door?"

The bite of the cold nips at my exposed ankles, and I shuffle past him like a wounded animal averse to the abuse of the outdoors.

He laughs again, closing it and leaving just us, the low sounds of the radio playing over the store's speakers, and the lingering cold settling around us like a fog over a lake in the early morning.

"I'm cold," I spit out like I'm not standing here with only my eyes peeking out from my layers of clothing.

"I gathered as much." He sighs again. "Come on, you. Let's get you warmed up."

Nicholas—Saint Nick of my nightmares—walks past me. I keep my arms crossed and wait until his steps disappear.

I could stand here and freeze. I could go back out in the cold, find a coffee shop that may or may not be open to the public yet.

Or...I could go to his fireplace.

Cold...or warmth.

I reach out for the handle, twist it, and one burst of wind through the cracked door is enough to have me slamming it closed, turning on my heel, and clambering back up the stairs.

At the kitchenette is Nicholas, pouring coffee and shaking his head with a smirk.

"Smart move," he mutters.

I cross the room without responding and sink back into his couch, reaching out to warm my hands by the fireplace.

Maybe if I just say nothing I can get warm enough to leave and not talk to him. I mean, what do I even say? How do I possibly tell him he's the catalyst for all the worst things in my life?

I smell coffee and find his hand extended out next to my ear holding a steaming mug of it.

"It'll keep your hands warm," he says.

I don't argue. I take it with a small "thank you," and my palms already feel better.

Nic meanders over to the big armchair catty-corner to the couch. It's made of quilted material with each square a different pattern of pine trees, fall leaves, and bears. It suits him.

"So, you gonna tell me why you ran off last night?" he asks, sitting down.

"We got to my inn. That's all."

"Right," he says with a chuckle. "That's all."

I watch him drink, finally able to take in all the similarities to the man I knew from my childhood. There are the strong hands with the bony wrists, now coated in wisps of arm hair; the plump, pink lips of a man too beautiful to exist and also be as rugged as him; the lingering ginger hairs in his otherwise graying beard; and the baby blue eyes that twinkle.

"Can I at least get your name?" he asks.

I blink a few times. I almost don't want to tell him. But, while I don't owe the dude a dang thing, he is letting me use his fireplace. And it's not like he'd remember me.

So I do.

"Birdie Mae," I say.

"Birdie Mae," he mouths silently. His face goes blank,

his lips parting slightly, like maybe he places me. But there's no way.

"I met you when I was younger," I continue. "You... helped me sneak a letter into Santa's pocket at the mall."

His bright eyes widen, and he laughs, so much cheer in every perfect vibration of it.

"Wow, yeah, that's right! You were the little girl who loved Christmas." I nod, curious how he remembers it so clearly. I know why I do, but him...why does he remember that day too? "And I...well, who was I to you in this narrative?"

"You're the man who ruined Christmas."

Then he isn't smiling anymore. His expression drops.

"What?"

"You said you hoped I would eventually hate Christmas," I say. "Like a curse." I know how petulant I sound, how dumb. "Christmas was...not good after I met you."

"Wait, what happened?" he asks. "I didn't do something, did I?"

"Yeah, you said I'd hate Christmas."

"That's all?"

"...it's complicated." I can't find the words again, and now I feel silly.

He nods, sips his coffee, and then gives a quick shake of his head.

"Fine. I won't press." He blinks. "Wow, small world, though."

"Wish it were bigger," I whisper.

He narrows his eyes, and I can't tell if he's upset or just trying to figure me out. Either way, I don't like it.

"So you're here in St. Rudolph to...?" he asks.

I look at the coffee and shrug. I don't want to talk to him.

"Have some fun on the side with the local bartender?" he asks with a quirk of his brow.

Nope. No. I'm not doing this today.

I exhale, twisting to gather my gloves from the seat next to me. "I wasn't going to sleep with you," I snap. Lies, but whatever; I'm angry. "And I don't need this teasing from *you*. Have a nice life, Nicholas."

I stand up again and exit the apartment with more conviction than last time, but he's following once more. All the way to the front door where my gloved hands do not have the fortitude to open the damn door with the wind whipping on the other side.

His voice comes from behind me. "Will you please stop taunting me with the door?"

I twist on my booted heel and tilt my head to the side. He's leaning against the counter with his hands cupping the mug. That lean…I know that lean so well. I picture it in my dreams and here he is, in the light of day.

Nic takes another sip from his coffee. It's haughty, if sips could be haughty. And then he sets it down on the counter.

"Okay, I said I wasn't going to press, but seriously, did I do something to you so many years ago? I just wanna make sure I wasn't…I don't know…a jerk, I guess."

"Do you think you were?" I ask.

"Was I?"

"What do you think?"

He laughs. "Why are you answering my questions with questions?"

"You're doing the same."

"Cute."

"Don't call me cute, Nicholas."

"Call me Nic. And why can't I call you cute?" he asks.

"Because I'm not supposed to like you," I say.

"Even though you showed up at my place at nine in the morning?"

"It's almost ten."

He's smirking at my insolence, and I can't help the little twitch at the edge of my mouth that enjoys the banter. And also how he looks at me.

It's weird—even though I'm teeming with anger, it's difficult to ignore some weird tug in my chest, like there's a pull between us. I can feel myself gravitating closer, the way I'm holding my breath waiting for the next sharp comment, the way his lips part slightly as his eyes roam down to my neck and up again.

Jesus.

"So, what are you doing in St. Rudolph, Birdie Mae?"

The way he says my name…

"I'm working," I say, shifting from one foot to the next trying to gain control again. "I write holiday books. I'm here for the wintery Christmas experience."

"Anything I'd know?"

I nod to the front counter. "Those."

Nic turns and glances over my books, one innuendo after another on display. His smile is so big.

"Wow, really?" he says. I can see his eyes darting over every cover. "That's amazing. You illustrated them too?"

"Yeah."

"I knew you had a future in writing after that letter." My stomach drops. Why does it sound like he's thought of me after that day? "Though, you got a weird thing for Santas?" He lifts an eyebrow.

"No!" I blurt out. Probably a bit too loudly because afterward all there is just the sound of the holiday music humming through the speakers.

"Okay, but you have a series of them, so…?"

"Money," I say.

"Nah, that's not it. You're not a sellout. I've read them, actually," he says, tracing a finger over one of the spines. It sends a shiver down my own. "Your books."

I try to lean against the doorframe in the same arrogant fashion he does.

"No you haven't."

"I have." His eyes flit to mine. "What, men can't read romance? They're good. You should be proud. But… well…the problem is they're dream Santas. Fantasy men."

I scuff my boot on the floor and mutter, "They're just books."

He lifts both eyebrows. "I think it's cleverly concealed baggage."

The nerve. The gall.

"It's not," I say.

"We've all got baggage, Birdie Mae. You tell me yours, I'll tell you mine." He repeats the same statement from last night, a deal I want no part in. Who knows what other holiday voodoo he can stitch into my life?

He pauses then clicks his tongue. "Alright then. I think there's only one solution here. Have you ever been to one?"

I snort. "A therapist? Try once a month."

"A mall Santa," he says with a chuckle. "Have you ever actually sat on Santa's lap and told him what you want? Maybe you've got unresolved childhood stuff."

"That's ridiculous."

I do, but that's beside the point.

"Is it ridiculous?"

"What do you want me to do?" I say, laughing despite myself. I can taste the bitterness on my tongue. "I'm thirty-one—I'm not going to sit on Santa's lap."

He raises an eyebrow. "Afraid you'd like it too much?"

My heart doesn't just skip a beat; it trips over itself entirely.

I narrow my eyes. He narrows his.

"I'll even go with you," he says.

"Why would you do that?"

"Solidarity. And I hate that maybe I ruined something as special as Christmas for you."

"Don't you have…I don't know…family to visit or… stuff?" I ask.

His face falls again, and he looks away. "I, uh, recently got divorced actually."

My face feels like the blood rushes out of it, and my stomach drops right down to the floor.

Well, I'm officially the worst.

Here he is beaten down, divorced, alone, and I'm breaking into his house.

"I'm so sor—"

He interrupts before I can finish my apology. "I could use some Christmas spirit."

"Even with Santas there?" I ask. "Aren't you president of the Hate Santa club?"

His eyes meet mine again, and they seem fierce. My whole body feels rigid, and my thighs clench closer together. That intensity could make a woman grab a mistletoe real quick.

"With you, maybe I wouldn't be."

How does he do that? I should be hating him, but then he's…like that.

"I'm here to write," I say with a shake of my head.

"No, you're here to get the Christmassy experience for these books. As a reader, I gotta make sure you get the perfect amount of Christmas cheer, and there's nothing more Christmassy than sitting on ol' Saint Nick's lap."

He smiles, dimples and all. My legs may as well be

mushy old fruit cake. How in the world did this man get divorced?

"A different Saint Nick, right?" I clarify. "Not sitting on your lap, am I?"

"You're funny, Birdie Mae," he says, "I like that about you."

At some point, he moved closer to me, because I'm pressed against the door and his familiar scent of pine and peppermint is intoxicating. My head is swimming, and I don't know the last time my stomach felt like it was going to fall into a pit, right down to my core that is clenching harder than ever.

I blink up at him. "You didn't answer my question."

Nicholas lets a slow, lazy smile grow on his face. His dimples pop. His eyes twinkle.

"You can do whatever you like with me."

I part my lips to say something, anything, but then I feel pressure against my butt, and when I turn, a lady is trying to open the door.

The bell dings above us as I step to the side and let her in.

I look up and Nicholas is at the counter, his lips upturned in a lopsided smile. "I'll grab my coat."

CHAPTER *five*

I CAN'T BELIEVE I'M IN LINE FOR SANTA. NOT ONLY THAT, but that I'm in line for a fake Santa I'm not dating with hot, nightmare Nicholas at my side whistling *Little Drummer Boy* in tandem with the mall's radio.

I haven't been this pissed about seeing Santa since... well, 1999.

Nicholas's whistles stop then start once more as the next classic holiday song rolls over the mall radio.

"Can you not?" I ask.

His thick gray eyebrows rise.

"Your whistling is beautiful like a bird's, Nicholas," some grandma coos behind him.

"Why, thank you, Betty," Nic responds with a wink.

It's subtle, a quick little motion like it was meant for her and only her, but I see it and it makes my chest grow warm. His twinkling eyes are like the cherry on top.

"Geez," I whisper under my breath through a forced laugh.

"What?" he asks. "She's a nice lady. Runs the bakery."

Nic then leans forward, the shadow from his height looming over me. It's not that he's super tall by any means. He's close to my brother-in-law's height, so probably a solid six feet, if I had to wager. But it's his presence…the sheer mass of him…

"So, what are you asking for?" he whispers, hot air against the shell of my ear.

I shiver and toss my head away from him.

"I'm not telling you."

"Awful lot of secrets between us, Birdie Mae."

"That's what happens when you're in line with a stranger," I whisper back.

Some kid chimes in beside us. "You shouldn't talk to strangers."

I look down, eyeing a kid about my nephew's age with hair that looks windswept even though we're in the middle of a toasty, un-windy mall. He has a cut above his eyebrow, and when he smiles, I can see two front teeth missing. He's a walking holiday song.

"Right you are, Cooper," Nic says.

"How do you know everyone?" I mutter under my breath before saying to Cooper, "Nic is a stranger. Should I not talk to him?"

Cooper gives me a toothless grin. "Oh, no, Mr. Nicholas is nice."

"Oh, great," I deadpan, throwing Nic a glare.

Nic chuckles to himself and goes back to whistling.

We walk through the ropes as the elves up ahead wave kids through one by one every couple minutes.

"Are you getting starstruck?" Nic asks when I'm finally next in line. I roll my eyes. "I mean, we're about to see *the Santa.*" He accentuates the name, as if it should trigger something more powerful in me. All I'm feeling is the lurch in my stomach at how close he is to my back right now. And how I wish he'd keep speaking warm breaths into my ear.

"But it's not Santa," I whisper low enough so Cooper doesn't hear. "Just a fake."

"That's no good for holiday spirit," Nic says, peering around me and checking out the fake Santa on his throne.

It's weird how Nic looks at him, as if inspecting who it is. He nods approvingly, and part of me actually feels a little bit better, but I don't know why. He knows everyone, so maybe he's looking out for the weird Santas? Then, right as the elf helper walks up to me, he steps one long leg over the dip in the ropes. "All you, Birdie Mae."

"Wait, where are you going? What about solidarity…" I start, but then she's unhooking the rope from its holder and looking from me down to little Cooper.

"Alright, kiddo," she says, throwing a thumb over her shoulder.

Cooper shakes his head with a grin. "Oh, she was in line first." It's a too-big smile that puts those two gums lacking teeth on full display. A grin like he's pleased as peppermint punch that an adult is in line with him for Santa.

The elf's eyes narrow.

"You're kidding," she deadpans.

"It's a tradition to visit Santa," I say with a shrug. It's not entirely a lie. Except my tradition seems to be sitting on their lap in private with far less clothing. This'll be a change for sure.

The helper elf rolls her eyes, but I sidestep her and let myself through with a barely audible, "Thaaank you."

I skip up the stairs and then it's just me and the jolly fat man.

All fake Santas are a mixed bag of possibilities. Some make excellent waffles and have gloriously real beards, and some have a lot of tattoos and a tongue made to fit a woman's nether regions.

This guy looks like the former because the second he sees me, I know his tongue can't possibly be made for pleasing women. He's too happy. Not enough edge. And definitely a bit older than my usual Santas.

"Ho ho—ho boy." Fake Santa's beaming face falls at the sight of me. "You'vegottabekiddingme."

"I want this less than you, I promise," I mutter as I climb the remaining two stairs to his throne and plop myself right onto his widespread thighs.

Fake Santa leans in, and I can smell the day on him. At first there's a hint of peppermint—as there should be for any good fake Santa—but after that initial hit, I recognize the unmistakable musk of a midafternoon Santa suit. I've washed far too many of them to know.

"And what do you want, little girl?"

"Listen, I'm just here to appease that man over there," I say with a nod in Nic's direction.

Nic is leaning against a pillar opposite Santa's throne, looking all the gorgeous man that he is. Hands in pockets, blue denim jacket with the sherpa fur around his neck, and groomed hair barely bothered by the dusting of snow we had on the way here. He's Mrs. Claus's wet dream.

"He looks like a younger me," Fake Santa says followed by a belly-clutching "Ho ho ho."

Thanks. Way to rub it in.

"You're much more charming than him, I promise," I say.

"Oh, that can't be true." Even through the disbelief, he's still smiling, keeping that Santa demeanor. It's actually endearing. He weirdly reminds me of Zack, my first Santa. It's his slightly crooked and bumpy nose. Unique, but offset by a set of straight pearly whites.

"So, what do you need?" Fake Santa asks. "A new pony? An engagement ring from your man over there?" I shake my head no with pursed lips. "Well then, let's go, chop chop, what's up?"

And yes, he does remind me of Zack, actually. It's the cadence in which he speaks. I'm instantly a bit more at ease.

"I'm honestly not sure," I say with a shrug.

"You know, normally kids just tell me what they want for Christmas, so how about we start there?" He tosses his head side to side, and something in the motion is kind. It's the red cheeks that seem like they've both had too much blush while also representing a very overheated man.

I laugh. "I don't know…world peace?"

"Are you not at peace?"

I'm again shaken by the similarities between him and Zack. He was all about peace and meditation. He even thanked the Christmas tree for its gifts, which made Anne refer to him as 'hippie Santa' for years. It's startling how much this man's voice mirrors the same sentiments.

"I'm just…well, it's always a bit of a lonely season, you know?" I continue.

Fake Santa is quiet before adding, "It doesn't have to be. I promise."

There he is again. Zack smiling right back at me. I could almost swear it.

And then a feeling comes over me. A feeling, then words—words suddenly bubbling out of me like hot volcanic lava that's been dormant in my soul this whole time. One second I'm nervous and the next I'm saying, "I'm sorry. For all I did. For all we went through."

"What?"

What, indeed. But I keep talking. It feels too right.

"No, shh, just let me finish," I say. "You remind me of my ex, and I'm having some kind of breakthrough, I think."

"Um…" He's shifting uncomfortably. I don't blame him, but I'm on his lap and I ain't going nowhere.

"Listen, Zack…"

No stopping this train now.

"Zack?"

"Zack, I'm sorry for breaking up with you the day after Christmas. It was snowing, which it never does in December in Georgia, and you were so excited to give me that record player and I told you I didn't want it. I did want it, actually. But I was confused and heartbroken about my dad, but I guess that's not new and…I'm sorry."

It all comes out so fast I don't even know how to inter-pret it myself. But something in my chest clicks into place, like a puzzle piece of my heart that was taken away years ago by The Curse and has now been reintroduced inside me.

Fake Santa blinks quickly. "Is that…all?"

It's like he's tiptoeing back into the conversation. Like maybe I've got a knife and I'm holding him hostage. But I'm not. Instead, I feel great. I feel relieved. Who knows, maybe women with knives feel that way too.

"Yes," I say, heaving out a long exhalation. "That's all."

"Okay, good," he grunts, definitely one hundred percent done with me. "Then off the lap, missy."

"Wait, don't I get a picture with you?"

"No."

With an exaggerated frown, I hop off his lap and give a small head nod to the sneering helper elf, shuffling my way through the ropes and out toward Nic. Only the sounds of Cooper squealing with joy behind me signal that the world is back as it should be. Except I feel…different. Better.

"How was it?" Nicholas asks.

His eyes are darting all over me, like maybe he's

checking for something to have changed. It has, but not on the outside.

"I...apologized," I say, blinking through my thoughts.

Nic refocuses on my eyes and slowly grins down at me with a barely visible dimple indention pressed like a thumbprint into his beard.

"You apologized?" he asks with a chuckle. "For what?"

I can't exactly tell him about Zack, or any exes. Last I checked, I agreed to be Vice President of the Santa Haters Club. Plus, his hand is now going for my arm, and I'm frozen in place as he plucks a piece of white Santa fluff from my coat.

I'd visit all the Santas to have that hand near me again.

"Stuff," I say. "I don't know. It honestly felt like therapy."

"Dang, I've been wasting money on a therapist when I could just get a Santa?"

"And to think, you've been hating them for no reason."

His jaw clenches and he shakes his head. "No, I think I have my reasons. But that one is one of the good ones. That's ol' Rick. Super-cool dude. Spearheads the Sunday farmers' market."

I nod slowly. Why'd he feel the need to check out who it was beforehand anyway? I don't ask. Instead, we exit the mall, the wind less chilling than it was before we went in. The sun has melted some of the snow, but not all. All in all, it's not too bad of a day.

"Well," Nic says with a clap of his hands. "Get everything off your chest?"

I shrug. "Some of it."

"Wanna do it again?"

I pause mid-step, peering up at him. And yet, it feels like he read my mind. Because that experience stitched back together part of my soul I wouldn't have gotten without Nic pushing me to do it.

"You're kidding," I say.

"I don't joke about Santa apologies."

"It's not—"

And then...my heart stops. Time stops. Everything stops as he turns to face me and slowly takes my chin between his forefinger and thumb, tilting my head up to him. It could be seen as a gentle, friendly gesture, but my sinking stomach wants to say otherwise.

It's simple, but it takes my breath away and makes my whole body freeze.

"Hey. You gotta clear out those Christmas cobwebs, Birdie Mae."

Our eyes lock for a moment, and his crystalline blues beam through me to melt me to my core.

I say nothing, and after a beat of silence, he lowers his hand again. But my heart still pounds like the hooves of reindeer in my chest.

"You...you gotta stop that," I say.

"Stop what?"

"Being...charming. I think."

That's the best I can come up with because I'm not supposed to have a beating heart for Nicholas. Not him. Not ever. And yet I'm standing here still trying to collect my thoughts from that weirdly sensual chin grab that makes me wanna douse myself in cold snow.

He chuckles. "I'll try my best."

"Ahem, how...how many more Santas could there be in this town?" I stutter out.

"Oh, Birdie Mae. I'm sure there aren't enough Santas for you, but we can try."

I smile, despite myself.

"Ass," I mutter.

He grins.

"Well, thanks for joining me, even though you totally abandoned me," I say, eliciting a small "Hey!" from him that keeps me grinning. I hate it. "But now I've got work to do."

"More Santas tomorrow then?" he asks.

I turn, the wind blowing through my hair, chilling my neck. It catches his hair as well, shifting the gray locks and ruffling his trimmed beard. I open my mouth then close it.

I had a great time, but…it's him. And he's…

"No," I finally say.

His eyebrows furrow.

"Oh, I thought…" he starts, almost more to himself than me. A whisper of a wish. "Why do you hate me so much again?"

I can't find the words. Would it even matter? And, if it did, how rational is it?

I'm an adult. I know Nic isn't some ethereal being who has the power to ruin everything, but the same girl who knows this is also the same one who swears—swears to all baker's dozen reindeer—that nothing was the same after him.

Because it simply wasn't.

"Something in me…thinks you wrecked my child-hood," I say. "And I can't seem to shake it just yet."

"Will you tell me why?" he asks. He looks so sad, and my heart breaks for him. But not as much as it does for myself.

"No. Just…I know it doesn't make sense, but…"

"Did you not get your Furby, Birdie Mae?" he asks. "Is that the issue here?"

My cheeks heat. Slow then quick and then all at once, just like a shattered dam releasing the memories in a flood.

"Wait…how…how do you remember that?" I ask.

Nic shrugs, like remembering something from twenty years ago is just something he does. Like, who *wouldn't* remember that detail?

"It'd be a shame if you didn't is all," he mutters.

"I didn't," I say, almost a whisper.

"You should have."

I can't wrap my head around this. I wanted that toy so bad. I know now Furbies were rare and basically unfindable that year. I sometimes wonder if Dad was on the hunt for one that night.

Nic is dredging up the past of a day I want so badly to forget.

"Stop," I say, almost a whisper. "You don't even know me."

"No," he says, taking a step forward. I take one back and he stills, his eyebrows furrowing as if I just slapped him. "But what if I told you I remember that day too?"

I can't feel my toes, and whether that's the snow around us or the feeling that maybe that day meant something to him too—good or bad—I'm not sure.

"What?" I squeak out.

"Funny how that works out, huh?" he says with a lopsided smile. Without the dimples, it seems forced and sad. "I ruined your Christmases, and you…had a different impact. A good one."

"You're just saying that," I say.

He tilts his head to the side, his eyebrows furrowing again.

"Is that so hard to believe?"

Is it true? Did we have completely different experiences that day?

"I…I gotta go."

I inhale, exhale, and turn on my heel to leave. I don't even say goodbye. I simply walk the one mile through the snow back to the inn where I'm comforted by silent words, a clacking keyboard, and absolutely no life-ruiners within the vicinity that can make me sick with longing at the mention of a creepy, bug-eyed, outdated toy I wanted twenty years ago.

The one I never got.

CHAPTER Six

THREE DAYS BEFORE CHRISTMAS

I saw Mommy kissing Santa Cl—

Before I can even reach my alarm, it is cut off by the sound of an incoming phone call. I grab the buzzing device and my sister's face stares right back at me, cheeky grin and all.

I groan into the phone. "My alarm is set for eight o'clock on the dot, which means it is ten o'clock on the dot where you are. Please tell me you don't have an alarm set to call me."

"Skipping the niceties, huh?" Anne says.

"They're reserved for sisters who respect time differences," I say, pulling the covers back over my head and taking a short roll so I'm wrapped up tight like a human burrito.

I swear this place will never get warm.

"So, I checked the weather in your area…"

"Of course you did," I mutter.

There's a split-second pause before she finishes with "…and it doesn't look like the snow is letting up any time soon."

My fingers poke out from under the sheet just enough to part the blinds on the window beside me. All I see is pure white fluff, a duplicate of yesterday. It must have snowed again overnight.

"Beem…" She inhales, and I can tell the typical mom thing is coming next. Anne was always really good at adopting the mom voice after our actual mom lost her ability to do so. "I'm getting worried."

"Anne. I'll be home for Christmas. Stop worrying."

"I *am* worrying!" Anne's voice is a low whisper, and I can hear floorboards on her end of the line creaking and the television in the background fading as she walks into another room. "Mom keeps calling asking for Daddy, and you're just so much better at dealing with this than I am."

The nerves in my chest feel like doom looming over me. Well, it can't catch me if I'm under the covers, so I try nestling myself further into the comfort of my quilted burrito.

"Responsible Beem doesn't want to come to the phone today."

"Birdies are not allowed to fly from the coop."

I open my mouth to say something but stop at the sound of knocking.

Wait, there's knocking at my door…?

I freeze, peeling back my covers bit by bit, layer by layer, until my eyes peek out toward the unmoving barrier.

"Beem? You there?" Anne asks.

"Someone just knocked," I whisper. "I'm sure it's just room service or something."

Then a low voice from the other side of the door says, "Room service, you say?"

Nicholas.

I bolt upright, my phone clattering to the floor in the process. The chill in the air hits me so harshly I instantly tug my quilt back up to my chin and over my shoulders, leaving me looking like the upper half of the Headless Horseman.

"Birdie Mae?" Nicholas says.

"How'd you find my room?" I call out.

"Dorothy and I go way back," he says through the door. "She told me which room you're in. Can I come in?"

"What?! No!" I yell. "Why are you here?"

There's a low rumbling chuckle, and I can just picture how his breath ruffles the whiskers of his graying beard.

"I'm trying to get you not to hate me," he says. "But I guess showing up at eight a.m. wasn't the best way to do that."

Heat rises in my cheeks.

It's only then that I hear the loud, almost tinny sounds coming from my phone.

"Birdie Mae?!"

Anne.

I lean over the side of the bed, still trying to remain as tightly coiled in my sheets as possible, and snatch the phone off the rug.

"Hey, can I call you back later?"

Anne is not having my nonchalance.

"Who is at your room this early, Birdie Mae?!" She practically squeaks.

"A local. I don't know."

I *do* know. I know exactly who this man is, and that's the problem.

"Oh, you better pinky-swear, double-dog-promise me we're gonna talk about this later."

"That doesn't even make sense, Anne."

"Call. Me. Back," she says through gritted teeth.

I hang up and sit there for a moment, trying to take in whatever the heck is going on here until I hear a small "Uh, hello?" from the handsome Christmas nightmare on the other side of the door.

"Hang on!"

I kick away the covers, ignoring the sting of the cold and running across the room to the desk chair where I threw my pants last night. I toss them on, tug on my college hoodie—squealing when my face gets caught because I fear dying from suffocation every time—then slide across the floor to unlock the latch and swing open the door.

Nicholas is leaning against the doorframe, doing that same kind of lean he does with one hand relaxed in his coat pocket like he's somehow earned the certificate on How to be Handsome from a local college. It's a cocky type of talent decorated with a half-smile, a raised eyebrow, and twinkling eyes. Yes, here he is, old Saint Nicholas with blue eyes and dimples ready to slay harder than a knight after a dragon. And holding a cup of coffee.

"So, coming to my room at eight in the morning is the way to make me not hate you?"

He shrugs. "You broke into mine yesterday."

"I had no idea that was your apartment," I say, a finger held up. "Very different."

"Well, I brought an olive branch. Err, coffee," he comments with a flick of his gaze down to the cup in his hand.

"For me?"

"For you."

When I stare at it for more than a couple seconds, he lets out a light chuckle. That dang laughing thing is almost just as dang warm and comforting as his dang sparkling eyeballs.

Dang dang dang.

He sighs. "Well, when you're done looking like you wanna kiss me or kill me—I honestly can't tell, but your face is definitely getting redder by the minute—put on some proper clothes, you," he says, nodding his head at me. "We've got another Santa to see."

"What?" I practically spit out.

"You wanted to, didn't you?"

"I...well maybe, but..."

I did, and I was even starting to consider going alone, but if he's here and he's looking delicious and he's offering coffee...

"Oh, come on," he croons, losing only an ounce of his swoon to be adorably boyish. It's maddening. "Give me a chance to redeem myself. I'm sure a younger Birdie Mae would like that."

A smile tugs at the edge of my lips. "She wouldn't, actually."

"Ruthless," he responds with a crinkle of his nose and a grin.

But even so, he doesn't move from my doorframe.

Though, with each passing second of raw silence, his cocky demeanor fades. His shoulders start to slouch, and his hand digs deeper into his pocket like his stiff arm is the only thing keeping him upright and keeping the coffee cup from overturning.

It's cute. It's endearing.

Dang it!

"Okay, let me put on a sweater," I say with a roll of my eyes. "But *one* Santa! That's it then I've gotta come back to work on stuff."

"Of course," he says. "Don't let me pull you away from your sexy Santas for too long."

Little does he know, I'm leaving one just to be with another. But that's beside the point.

I swipe my beanie—the one with the puff ball on top —to sling on top of my unwashed hair then I'm suddenly hit from behind. I turn on my socked feet to find one of my thick coats on the floor beside me, slack from the impact. Then a second comes flying toward me, hitting my hip and then the ground, all from the hands of Nicholas.

When we make eye contact—me with the glare of a spoiled child on Christmas Day and him with the mischief of the elf who caused such disappointment—he's grinning from ear to ear. His dimples are barely hidden beneath that beard and pink cheeks.

"I mean, you need two coats, right?"

I point a finger to the door. "Out, mister. I'll meet you downstairs."

He gives a small shrug, places the cup of coffee on the side table near the door, and surprisingly does exactly as I ask.

The moment he leaves, I take in the silence before crossing over to my phone to dial my sister back. She'd call the police if I didn't, I swear.

Anne answers before the first ring even ends and asks, "Okay, who was that?"

I'm not even sure where to start with this one, so I tell her it was the innkeeper returning my computer charger from last night.

I don't tell her we're going to visit a fake Santa, and I definitely don't tell her I'm hanging out with an attractive man who looks like Santa as well.

Because I can't imagine what she'd say, and I don't want to.

I know what I'm doing is wrong.

But that doesn't mean I'm stopping.

———

"Where are you taking me hostage today?" I ask.

We're trudging back toward the main downtown area. It feels so old world in this town. There aren't any cars because the roads haven't been plowed yet. The only sounds are my totally unsexy heavy breathing as I struggle through snow, the shifting of the ice, and occasional jingling bells coming from who knows where. I swear it's like a soundtrack here.

"There's a Santa in the square," Nic says. "I think it's Tim's gig."

"Oh, Tim," I say, the words coming out like more of a coo. "The guy from the bar?"

"That's the one."

"Do you like bartending?" I blurt out.

He laughs. "I like talking to people. It gets me out of the house."

"No family?" I ask. He quirks an eyebrow. "I mean, uh, that...sorry. Divorce, I know."

"Yeah, but also"—he points a thumb to his chest—"orphan. So you pretty much hit the nail on the head."

"Wow, I ask the worst questions."

"Well at least you didn't call me Orphan Annie."

"Good lord, that's horrible."

"Red hair and an unfortunate situation," he says, kicking a small pile of snow. "Kids are cruel."

"Geez, that's next level."

"Admit it, I could see the insult forming on your lips," he says with a wink, which immediately sends me into high heaven. It's cruel to be that good at winking.

It's that flirtatious high that makes me ask, "You're looking at my lips?"

I shouldn't be flirting with the enemy, and yet...and yet...

His voice is low and delicious when he responds, "Always, Birdie Mae."

God, his responses are like a sigh of relief. I don't think I could have more jitters in my chest unless I was given a direct IV of melted down candy cane. I have to look away, but I know I can't hide how red my face is, not even if I bury myself in my scarf.

"So," I continue, "you're saying you want me to sit in your buddy's lap?"

Nic laughs.

"Right. Well, Tim is harmless," he says. "Been doing the whole Santa thing for thirty years or so."

I laugh and muse, "First Rick, now Tim. Are you friends with every Santa in town?"

He doesn't say anything for a second, but his posture gets notably more rigid. His footfalls are more purposeful, and his stare looks like a reindeer in headlights, but with an edge of anger, like he's the deer that would totally break your windshield just to spite you.

I don't like the look, but at the same time, I can feel my nipples harden underneath my three layers of shirts, so there's that.

"Not every Santa," he says. It's like Nic is trying to be chill, but the dude has no chill right now.

I shouldn't poke the bear but, hey, when in Rome...

"Oh, okay, so you're just *scared* of Santas," I tease. "Right. Got it."

"I'm not...no." He slowly drags out the last syllable, his mouth quirking up into a smile. "I'm not *scared* of Santa, Birdie Mae."

"Sure you're not," I say. "I get it, though. A man with a mysterious bag? Squeaky pleather boots walking behind you at night? Claims to see you when you're sleeping? I shudder to imagine it too."

Nic laughs, leaning back as if the sound overtakes him. I like to watch his chest move as he does it. And after a second, it almost seems like he dislikes that he's laughing, as if the weight of his disdain for Santa should overpower every ounce of happiness he wants to have. But it doesn't. He's practically *ho-ho-ho*-ing himself.

When he's done, he bites his bottom lip, inhaling and then exhaling as he silently kicks a pile of snow in front of us like some shy kid trying to figure out what else to do with all his bottled-up energy.

"You could write horror, you know," he says.

"I'll consider it. So, what's wrong then?" I ask. "Why are you weird about Santa?"

Nic glances over at me, lip still captured between his beautifully capped white teeth. The beard hair close to his plump lip is short and almost stubbly. It has a hint of his former ginger color, and that makes my stomach twist in a weird way I instantly like and hate.

"Seriously, go on," I coax.

"Tell me yours, I'll tell you mine," he teases.

I roll my eyes, trying to regain my own composure. Now it just feels ridiculous to tell this man who is far too talented at making my heart flutter with just a single closed eye that I'm a Santa connoisseur. So I don't. I can't.

"No, thanks," I say through a laugh.

"Then no answers for you."

"Don't want them anyway."

Except that's a massive stupid horrible lie.

I'm a writer, and if there's any sure thing about writers,

it's that we're nosy. I'm super-stalker-level nosy about Nicholas's baggage.

I want to know his secrets.

Bad.

———

Tim's lap is far less comfortable than fake Santa number one. In fact, he's smaller than a Santa should be, like maybe he skipped out on a few months of the whole-milk-drinking needed to build the typical fluffy physique. But it doesn't seem to matter much since everyone in line is too distracted by everything else going on.

It's a weird vibe in the square. Not only is there an elaborate gingerbread house set up, but the helper elves are buff here—like seriously, weirdly buff. They stand with crossed arms that stretch their bright green t-shirts. Like a holiday Chippendales.

It's too crowded, even more so than the mall. I spot Cooper also in line, waving at me like some serial killer lunatic with his two missing teeth. Harsh to call a kid a crazy man, I know, but it's a sight to see. He looks nuts. However, even he flinches a bit when the buff elves walk past.

I'm a little less concerned with their intensity after spending time next to Nicholas's incessant whistling. I nudge him in the side and pointing out the buffest elf walking past.

"Rate him from 1 to 10," I whisper.

"That's Joe," Nic whispers back. "Solid 11."

"Yeah?"

"Oh definitely."

Before I know it, I'm back sitting on a fake Santa lap—

Tim's—shifting and trying to find a place where my bony butt and his bony leg can puzzle piece together. It's no good.

Conveniently for me, he's kind. Just as kind as he was two nights ago, which he surprisingly remembers.

"Get that eggnog you wanted?" He winks. I don't try to decipher the hidden meaning, at least not while I'm on his lap.

"Yes, but I asked for less of the extra liquor after seeing you fall over."

He chortles a cute little laugh. "Smart girl. So, what can I do ya for? Or are you just here for some weird kicks?"

I trust this little weirdo, and I guess I am here for some type of kicks. But he seems okay with it, and that's all the reassurance I need to look him dead in the eye and ask, "Can I pretend you're my ex and apologize to you?"

After only one second of shock—because he'd be crazy not to have any at all—Tim quickly composes himself and nods solemnly. Then he says, "Be my guest, ma'am."

Wow, easy enough.

I feel the air settle over me as I try to block out the peering eyes around us—the kids clambering through the line to get a closer look, the helper elves standing sentry, and Nicholas doing his infamous lean against a park tree— and I focus. I focus on exes of Christmas past and their gentle smiles, specifically...Frank's. Yes, Frank from three years ago, the older Santa who was admittedly far out of my usual age range. I remember how he smiled with his naturally crinkled nose and Elvis-like lips. It was a nice smile with a kind heart. Like Tim.

"I'm sorry for breaking up with you after the New Year's ball dropped...it was a particularly bad Christmas.

For me. For my mom. Don't ask. But you didn't deserve to have me come in and mess it up."

"I'm sure I understood," Tim says, playing along.

Thank you.

I let out a small laugh. "I'm sure you did, but I'm still sorry."

It's silent, the same type of silence that washed over me with Santa number one, with the same sense of comfort as well. The same feeling of relief, the puzzle piece locking into place.

"Feel better?" Tim asks, breaking me from my reverie.

I nod. "I do."

He smiles, and the sounds of the square come rushing back in. People talking. Snow crunching. Music playing. I even spy little Cooper by the lamp post giving me a subtle thumbs-up. It makes me smile.

"You know, Nic always liked interesting women," Tim suddenly says. I glance at him as he's mid eyebrow waggle.

"Oh, we're not…" Not what? Flirting? Into each other? Honestly, I'm not so sure anymore, so I don't correct him. "I mean, uh, thanks?" I say with a breathy laugh.

"Glad to see him out again. He deserves it," Tim continues. "But how'd you convince him to get out here?"

I glance around. "At a Santa gathering?"

"Well, yeah, in the square," he says with an almost mournful laugh. "After last year, I just thought he'd avoid it forever."

"What happened last year?" I ask. Because I can feel something I need: Nicholas's secrets, right on the tip of Tim's tongue.

"Oh, you know."

"Do I?!" I say, probably too quickly. Too insistently. Too…weirdly. In fact, I know it's too much because Tim doesn't respond with anything more than narrowed, curious eyes.

"He didn't tell you?" he asks.

"Should he have?"

Play it cool, play it cool.

But I'm desperate for information. Slowly being starved of the truth.

Tell me tell me TELL ME.

Tim cringes. "Listen, if you don't know, it's probably for the best."

"Wait, what happened?" I ask.

"I don't think I should say…"

A booming voice that is neither mine nor Tim's—I know because I'm wildly looking between his two eyes—yells, "NEXT!"

It's Joe, the macho elf who waits for nobody. His beefy hand is wrapping around my upper arm, pulling me off Tim. I flex my legs to keep my calves tucked underneath Tim's skeleton thigh.

"Tell me!"

"Lady, we've got a line," the buff elf says.

"Tim!" I plead, but—and I kid you not—Tim nods at the elf bodyguard like he's the freaking Godfather. He gives one single head nod to the bulking holiday elf who then tucks his hands underneath my armpits and lifts me off his knee like I'm a sack of potatoes.

I would feel more guilty for causing a scene, but I don't have time because Nic is already meeting us at the ropes with his hands braced on the metal pole, eyes bolting from me to the elf like I'm some cage fighter who got a bit too wild in the ring.

"Don't bring her back, Nic," the buff elf says, dumping me over the ropes and into his arms full-on bride style.

I'm already wiggling. Mostly because his wonderful hands are on me and it's putting my nerves on edge.

"I could take him!" I say back, probably getting a bit too caught up in the moment as Nic gently lowers my feet to the ground, keeping a tight hand on my shoulder as if steadying me. His touch is warm, seeping through all my heavy layers to my skin, which burns for more.

"Are you picking fights with Tim, Birdie Mae?" he asks with a laugh.

"No," I say like a petulant child. "But I'm gonna fight his buff elf." I shake off Nic's hand from my shoulder on instinct and instantly feel weird that I did. And I feel weird that it makes me feel weird.

"Let's not fight John Cena and Grandpa Skeletor today, yeah? You've got writing to do." Nic turns away from the Santa display before crooking his arm and proffering it toward me. "Come on."

I glance at the arm and back up to him. I want to deny him the chance at being a gentleman, but his lopsided smile and dimples are like two siren songs, and I'm just a lost sailor at sea.

"Fine. But I'm only going because I'm behind on my deadline," I grumble.

"Of course."

I take Nic's outstretched arm, placing my hand in the crook of it, and silently curse myself.

It's irritating how nice it feels to touch him, how warm he is, and how easy he is to joke with. His scent no longer feels taunting, but instead welcoming, like the pine and peppermint reminds me more of home than a bad memory.

So I keep my feet moving forward and exhale the feelings for him—the flutter in my heart, the buzzing that reaches all the way down to my stomach, the second voice between my thighs that practically yells for him.

Shut up, lady bits.

I focus instead on my feet and the freeze that comes through the crunching snow.

At least I do until I see a directional sign pointing toward the square we're now leaving. And then it reminds me…

"Hey Nic?"

"Hm?" His respond is a low rumble that sends my heart racing again.

No, focus.

"Tim mentioned he was surprised to find you at the square," I say.

Nic's jaw twitches. "Did he."

"Yeah…are you the leader of the Square Haters club too?"

I can feel the tension break as he smiles.

"Something like that," he says. "I, uh, got into a bit of an altercation last year."

An altercation? Oh god, did he fight someone? Am I walking arm-in-arm with a man who picks fights?

You know, I should be less turned on by that fact…

"Altercation?" I ask. "How delightfully vague."

"Well, if we're keeping secrets…"

And then the dang man winks at me again.

I'm gonna be a melted snowflake on the ground if he keeps that up, so instead I bite my lip and keep walking in silence.

We walk back through downtown, passing the toy store, the pub, and finally the bookshop with his apartment above it—the same bookshop with my own creations displayed in the window. I glance at the sidewalk ahead of us instead, avoiding them.

"Huh," Nic says.

"What?"

"You always look away when we pass your books. Are you ashamed?"

"No."

"So why don't you look at them?"

"I…have a weird relationship with them. I don't know…" I consider for a moment telling him exactly why they suck this year, why I'm okay being the VP of the Santa Haters club. It's difficult to like your Santa products when they remind you of your ex who broke your heart. But all I say is, "They're dumb, I guess. Now that I think about it."

He stops mid-walk. "Birdie Mae, do you really believe that?"

I pause in response. Hard not to with my hand still looped in the crook of his arm.

"Shouldn't I?" I ask.

"No." His face is blank, and I can tell in that one gesture that he isn't joking at all. "I think it's really cool, actually."

I tug on his elbow, my hand still warm in the crease. "Whatever, come on."

"No, really. I can't believe that same girl who wrote letters now writes books."

I pause. "How do you remember all that?"

"I'm telling you, that day meant something to me."

My chest feels like it constricts.

"I…" I can't think of anything. What he's saying seems so genuine, but also…so contradictory to how I've felt about him for so many years. "You know, for an author, I'm bad at words."

He bites his lip and rolls his eyes with a smile. "Sorry. Maybe we need more Santas."

"For what?"

"To handle all that baggage you're carrying."

"Oh, shut up," I say, giving him a light shove. It feels right in the moment, but the second after I do, I feel guilty. Like a younger Birdie Mae would be disappointed that I'm getting along with him and joking, touching him like I am and finding excuses to touch him more.

"So, are the Santas helping?" he asks with a smile. "Are you getting stuff off your chest? Selfishly, I'm hoping you hate me less."

I shake my head, lifting my chin in faux defiance. "I could never."

Except…my stomach churns when I say that. It feels wrong.

And I see a little bit of his expression drop, so subtly it could almost be missed. I feel…bad. The downward tug at the edge of his lips, the loss of that twinkle in his eye…

I don't like seeing him sad.

And all at once, without warning, a thought hits me like a snowball in the face.

Oh no.

I might actually like *Nicholas Ryan.*

The man who was the catalyst for so many horrible Decembers. The Cursebringer. The Grinch who stole all my Christmases. It's wrong. It's horrible.

And yet, when he looks at me with one eyebrow raised in curiosity, my heart pounds and I wish I could find out how soft his lips really are under that beard.

Oh no no no.

After a moment, Nic barks out a laugh, and I can't help but watch his Adam's apple move with the gesture. I wonder if he can read my mind, but instead he shrugs and says, "A man can hope."

I swallow and look down to the ground.

He has a sense of humor. And I like it. I like him.

"So, what about you?" I ask, hoping to clear my thoughts and come to something more rational.

"Well, I don't hate you, for starters."

He doesn't hate me.

Not what I needed to hear right now, Nic.

"No," I say. "How's that whole Santa hate thing going?"

"Oh. That," he says. "Uh, splendidly." He sidesteps a melting snow puddle, giving me a small nudge that helps me avoid it as well. Such a gentleman move that has my stomach dropping once more. This man is going to be the death of me. "Had time to make a voodoo doll at the last visit we made."

"You're so morbid."

"What would you rather me do?"

"I don't know. Not be unhappy, I guess?"

Nic looks down at me, the slow smile spreading on his face, and suddenly I'm smiling back and I feel so dumb because he's just so handsome and I'm just so stupid.

"Birdie Mae, are you telling me you care about my happiness even a little bit?"

My brain keeps screaming, STOP SMILING AT HIM, YOU GOON. But I can't. It's spreading slow and steady across my face like some parasite creeping from his being into me.

"I…no." I laugh. "Shut up."

He glances over my shoulder. Then his face falls.

I follow his look and turn.

There's a whirl of white coming right at us. We have a split second to react, but I'm not fast enough. He is, though, grabbing me around the waist and pulling me out of the way.

The punching, *plomp*ing sound of hardened snow hits the lamp post behind us.

Then a second snowball flies by, hitting the same spot but just a bit closer.

"Uh-oh, we gotta get out of here," Nic says, his arm unfurling around me only to land on my lower back, edging around to clutch my sides. I haven't had a hand rest in the divot of my hip like this in forever. I mean, sure, Stephen did, but not like this, not with this type of protection in it. Plus, I can feel the pressure of his hand as it clutches my side tighter. It's downright *erotic*.

I'm too baffled by the feel of his ungloved hand on my double layers of coats that I dumbly ask, "What? Why do we need to get out of here?"

"Snowball fight," he says, nodding toward the area behind me as he narrows his eyes and sneers, "Cooper."

"Cooper? What? But Cooper seems super nice..." I start to say, but oh how wrong I am. Neither of us notice the third snowball barreling right toward my face until it's too late.

Poompf.

And then I'm cold. My cheeks practically burn. The remnants of the snowball that hit my face break apart to crumble down to my neck and into my scarf, singeing that with cold as well.

There's silence—not even a crunch of boots—followed by a small, weak, sad little, "Oh no."

I look across the street, and there he is. Little Cooper. Surrounded by neighborhood kids who look stunned.

"Cooper..." one kid voice says, his tone fading into nervousness. "You hit a grown-up."

It's the same voice I used whenever Anne would try to wake up Dad too early on Christmas morning. I can still remember the grumbling bear noises he'd make. Looking back now, I know he would exaggerate them just to appear extra scary, but back then I had no clue. We were terrified. Daddy would always raise his arms up and claw his hands, yelling, "I'M THE ABOMINABLE SNOW MONSTER!" He'd chase us around the house until Momma told him he was going to wake the neighbors. She'd be laughing too, though.

Christmases were good then.

But now, as I stand beside Nic facing the terrified kids on the opposite side of the street behind their forts, I see the same sense of dread in their eyes.

Nic takes a step forward, shaking his head.

"Oh, buddy, you're in for it now."

Then the mood shifts. Because Nic yells. Yells—like a war cry.

And it's my dad all over again. Goofy but scary as the kids across the street scream out of fear and happiness and sheer holiday spirit.

My heart swells as Nic drops to the ground, bare-handing that cold snow like a mountain man forged from the ice. I'm in awe of him, watching him push it up, letting the flakes fluff up into his gray beard, streaking it with white snow.

He pauses, turning to look at me with a lifted eyebrow.

"Well, you gonna help, Birdie Mae?"

"Am I gonna..." I stammer out words, but I don't make it far before another snowball hits my face.

And it's cold. So so cold.

"Why, I oughta..." I say with a borderline Muppet-like fist shake.

"Let's get revenge!" Nic yells. The kids across the street cackle. They aren't scared anymore.

I fall to the snow-padded ground and get to work.

Because I do want revenge. I really do. But suddenly

not on Nic—on Cooper instead. Yes, *Cooper* is the one going down.

I muscle up some snow, compacting it into balls as quick as I can while Nic makes a fort-like barrier.

It's us against these kids.

And then we're tossing and getting things thrown at us. I can barely see, my cheeks are sore from the cold, and I'm shaking, but I'm laughing and throwing and then other adults start to join us. Even Dorothy from the inn waddles her way out and over to our side of the street with a shovel, which honestly just seems cruel, but it works to throw extra sheets of snow at them, no matter how haphazard or wild.

But even with the few of us adults trying to throw what we can, these kids are crazy.

I mean, absolutely nuts, you know?

They chant at us, voices rising like we're in some freaking *Lord of the Flies* nightmare, and they've got energy I just don't know if I ever had at that age.

Snowballs here and there. Snow darts. You don't think that's possible? Trust me, it is, and it happened. I think at one point even I was yelling, and Nic looked at me with some quirky smile and I just...well, I melted more than the snow, I think.

Then out of nowhere, our fort is down, and we're staring into the eyes of the enemy across the road.

We've suddenly lost, and Nic knows it.

He stands, stepping over the sorry lump that was our fortress with his hands in the air. Dorothy and I are gasping at his sacrifice. How brave. If he's their war prisoner, is it permanent? Will they let us visit?

Slowly, once he crosses the street, I see him outstretch his arms and fall backward, compressing their fort under his weight. They explode into happy kid squeals, some clearly a little bit upset but not enough to care because they pound him with haphazardly made snowballs.

Nic starts making snow angels on the ground, and the kids are already asking for a rematch as he's shaking his head, laughing.

It's cute. Too cute.

"I will not be bullied!" he yells.

I cross the street, plopping down beside him on the snow.

"Too many bad memories?" I tease.

He grabs my hand and pulls me closer to him. My chest flutters. He's on his back and I'm leaning on my side, propped up on my elbow next to him. I could look down at him all day.

"You try existing as a redhead in the nineties," he says with a wink.

That dang wink. And the snow, the way he's lying there like the hero of the day. A few strands of his hair are askew and to the side. I find myself reaching out to move them, lightly tracing the edge of his hairline to shift it back in place, and he's reaching out to put some of my loose hair behind my ear as well. It sends shivers through me.

"Thanks for leading us to a non-victory," I say.

Ugh, ew. I want nothing more than to hate myself for it. For the cheesiness of it all. For being such a cliche. I want to, but I don't. Because he's smiling up at me with those pearly whites and shrugging.

"All for you, Birdie Mae."

All for you.

How is this man so charming? How is he both kind and infuriating? And why is it rubbing me in just the right way?

His eyes drift from mine and down to my lips.

I inhale sharply.

And then, he leans in. My heart races. He's going to kiss me. I just know it. And I want it. I can feel his warm breath, smell the hint of minty toothpaste, and I start to close my eyes.

I realize at the very last minute, as his face veers upward to my forehead, that I miscalculated the situation because instead he places his warm, whiskered beard to my forehead.

And my chest lurches a bit.

I gulp, my heart feeling like it's both watery and mushy like the snow clumped in my gloves and scarf.

I feel so dumb. Sure, partially because I misjudged the kiss, but also because I feel…a thing. For him. Again.

No.

He lowers his face back down to my eye level, and I can still feel the warmth of his kiss lingering on my hairline, rushing down to my cheeks, my chest, and my stomach.

Nic smiles, and I see his tongue lick his own lips. My body reacts in kind. My thighs clench tighter, and my hands grip his sweater hard before I even think about it.

His eyebrows rise.

"Birdie Mae, are you blushing?"

"Oh, get over yourself, Nicholas," I say, rolling my eyes with a forced smile.

He laughs, the magic in the air breaking. He was messing with me. And, because I'm a bully, I push him back into the snow when he tries to sit up, which only makes him laugh harder.

Cooper bounds over with his toothy—or lack thereof, I guess—grin, holding out his hand to shake mine in some form of truce.

We all call it a day and we don't make promises for tomorrow. But somehow, I know I'll see Nicholas in the morning because he watches me with dazed eyes as I close the door to the inn, following behind Dorothy to dry off.

That laugh of his stays with me the rest of the night. When I'm eating dinner with Dorothy, when I'm writing, when I'm doodling potential illustrations… Sure, they're supposed to be sexy Santas, but they're really just renderings of Nic.

And my Santas have never looked this sexy.

CHAPTER seven

I saw—

I set my alarm extra early to get in some work. The words flow so easily. The illustrations, which I normally save for the spring, are rushing through my fingertips, begging to be put on paper. I'm addicted to the sensation. I'm still deep in the groove when my room's landline rings. I tug it to my ear, and something tells me it won't be Dorothy.

"The Christmas Eve Eve parade is today," Nic's voice says. "There's another Santa there if you're interested."

I hate that my heart rate pumps up a step with each word he says, like a car revving its engine. *Oh my god, does Nic now rev my engine?!*

I glance down at my dad's watch sitting on the desk beside me. It's almost eight a.m.

"How do you wake up so early?" I ask.

"Aren't you the one who answered the phone?"

I smile, wrapping the curling phone cord around my finger.

"I'm working. It's different. I could have been sleeping," I say.

"But I knew you wouldn't be." I can practically hear him grinning. "So, another Santa today?"

"It's starting to feel like Groundhog Day here," I say.

Nic barks out a laugh, and I can just imagine his beaming playful smile.

"Try living here year-round. Those Christmas lights never come down."

"Oh yeah?"

"Yeah." His words are slow, like a coda leading into a warm silence.

I float in it, this newly unspoken thing between us, spurred on by a simple kiss on the forehead. I settle into it like a fireside blanket on this snowy day. But then I hear my cell phone buzzing on the desk, and Anne's reliable face is there as usual. Right on the dot.

I cringe when I mute the call and send her to voicemail, telling myself I'll call her back.

"So, parade, Birdie Mae?" Nic asks through the phone.

I love it when he says my full name, like he's presenting me a gift wrapped up in a velvet bow.

"When is it?" I ask.

"Whenever you want to leave."

It's a non-answer, one that no doubt guarantees we meet up sooner rather than later. I accept with a "Let me shower and get ready."

"Meet you out front in an hour," he says.

I hang up then call Anne back; she's trying to decide whether her kids need one or two additional stocking stuffers—I tell her twenty to be cheeky and then she asks why I'm in such a good mood, but my mind is wrapped up in the gift that is Saint Nicholas. Not even her telling me I should book a flight for tomorrow dampens my mood.

Especially not when Nic appears at the inn's doorstep, arm outstretched for me to take one hour later.

And take it I do.

We make it to the parade by ten, and it is filled with thrown candy canes captured by kids, the local high school marching band, excessive floats based on different holiday movies, dancing people dressed as reindeer doing the Macarena for some reason, and then finally…parade Santa.

And yet the only thing I keep thinking about throughout all of it is how Nic will randomly touch a hand to my lower back to guide me through the crowds or how our fingers ghosted past each other when we reached for the same tossed candy cane.

Nic and I can't stop touching each other. That's the simple fact of it all.

His hand finds its way to my hip as he repositions me to move past. It's an excuse to touch me; I know it is. I would call him out on it, but then it'd give him permission to tease me, and I'm just as desperate to have my back pressed against his chest when the final horse-drawn carriage clops by.

The crowds disperse, and I immediately miss his warmth at my back. I turn toward him, and he throws me a wink.

I am so done for.

A kid rushes past me to get the last of the fallen candy, pushing me into Nic's chest because OF COURSE THAT HAPPENS TO ME.

I try to balance myself by gripping the back of Nic's neck. I hear him inhale sharply at the motion.

Our faces aren't even one inch apart, and his mouth twitches at the edges.

"Using any excuse to get close to me?" he asks.

I bite my lip and test the waters. "Enjoying it too much?"

His hooded eyes look down at me as he growls. "You have no idea, Birdie Mae."

Holy Mother Mary...

I could kiss him now, and I don't have to say it out loud to know he wants to as well. But should I? Is it right? Would younger Birdie ever forgive me?

I don't have time to consider. I don't want to. I want this. I want him.

So I take a leap and lean forward.

And then another kid attempting to get by nudges between us, splitting us apart.

Nic's hand goes up to rub his neck, and he lifts his chin in the direction of the Santa.

"Ready?"

I nod and walk beside him.

I worry the moment is over, but then he loops one pinky into mine—something so purposeful it can't possibly be misconstrued as a hand graze—and I let him. As we walk, I curl the rest of my hand into his as well, hoping he can't feel my pulse beating wildly through my fingertips because *ohmygod kill me now.*

Nic escorts me to the end of the parade where a makeshift Santa's workshop, complete with a large golden seat, awaits the parade Santa. A line is already forming behind a set of ropes, so we file in at the back.

Surprise, surprise: Cooper is already there, hands on hips.

"Wanna lose again?" Cooper taunts. I stick my tongue out at him as Nic holds me back.

"Let me at 'im," I jokingly whisper, and Cooper giggles the cute little kid type of giggle.

The line goes quickly with Cooper and Nic whistling

Christmas tunes together, all while Nic discreetly rubs his thumb over mine, a secret caress hidden in the comfort of his jacket pocket, which my hand has nestled its way into.

I try to focus on anything else, but that one motion is enough to make my nipples hard and my mouth feel so dry. I've never felt so anxious for the unknown, not with any Santa. So I try, best as I can, to listen to their whistles in silent torture—Cooper's a bit more like squeaky humming breaths—until finally, it's just me and Santa. Or Sam, as Nic says, because apparently he knows this guy too. He does squint at him for half a second, like maybe he is protecting me from the potential lies in the professional liar's eyes.

"It's just Santa, Nic," I say. "Go do your dumb leaning thing."

"I don't do a lean," he says with a scoff.

"Yeah you do."

I point at an oversized candy cane, biting my tongue as he smiles that cocky grin of his but feeling instantly uneasy once our hands disconnect.

Will we continue where we left off once I'm done with Santa? Will it be awkward?

It takes me a second to realize he doesn't leave right away. Instead, Nic takes a step toward me. He stops right at my forehead, planting a soft gentle kind of thing there right below my hairline.

I close my eyes. I could live in the comfort of his forehead kisses. I let the warmth from his scratchy beard radiate through my face. It's nice against the snowy day. His peppermint smell is nice. His nearness is nice.

I realize my eyes have been closed for too long, and when I finally open them again, he's beaming from ear to ear. Then Nic puts those hands back in his coat pockets, lifts his eyebrows, and walks off right as I'm stepping past the workshop attendant like I'm floating on air, onward to Santa number three: Sam.

Sam's got a decent look, but it's definitely parade Santa level. It's meant to be seen from far away. His fake beard shifts ever so slightly against his lips, and I can obviously make out the thin white strings attaching it over his ears. Santa number three seems tired, and I guess I would be too if I were waving to a crowd from a float for an hour only to be put on display for screaming kids immediately afterward.

"Hello, and what do you want for Christmas?" he asks me with a dull tone.

This dude is totally in the groove. I don't even know if he notices I'm me and not a five-year-old child, but oh well. I'm feeling this moment. The high from that forehead whatever kiss from Nic…it was wonderful and exciting, like a buzz starting at the tip of my head and moving down to my toes, sizzling the holiday spirit over me.

I glance over at him now, doing his little not-lean lean against the giant candy cane that's twice his height and stuck in the ground. He must lean a bit too much because it starts to shift and he stumbles, trying to regain his balance.

I can't help but laugh.

And I realize it's time.

"I want to do a quick apology if that's alright," I say to Sam.

"Hm, what?" I think Sam finally realizes who is sitting on his lap and that I am, in fact, not a child. "Wait, what?"

"An apology," I clarify.

"Oh, okay, uh…lady, what do you want to apologize for?"

"Stephen," I say, and the moment the name leaves my mouth, I can feel it melting like a forgotten snowflake on my tongue. "I wanna apologize to Stephen. Can you… pretend to…"

His face scrunches, and I realize I won't be as lucky with this Santa as I was with Tim.

"Uh, never mind," I say. "I wanna apologize to Stephen. I think I expected too much from him. I thought he was the one. I wanted him to be *it*, and he just wasn't. I'm sorry for pushing him to move in with me."

"Well, that's…" Sam seems more confused than anything else, but that makes sense. "That's a good apology."

"Yeah," I say proudly. The ultimate apology. The one I needed. "I think it is."

And I get up, feeling the relief flow through me, the piece of me lost a few weeks ago finally locking into place, and I pat fake Santa number three on the shoulder, bypassing the rope attendee and making my way right up to Nic, who I grab by the hand and drag away from the now fallen candy cane as he distantly yells, "Sorry!" all through muddled laughter.

We stop for hot chocolate at the booth set up near the pop-up workshop. After we order, Nic fishes out one of the giant marshmallows from his mug and plops it into mine.

"A gift?" I ask.

"Yes," he says with his chin tilted up in pride, but only for a second before it falls. "Aaand I just realized that now your drink has my messy finger germs in it…which I definitely didn't think about beforehand. Sorry."

Nic was grinning until now. In fact, he radiated confidence, but now he has a bit of a falter in his step. I wish I knew what he was thinking, why he is being a little more uncomfortable than usual, like a man nervous on a first date.

Wait, is this a date?

As we walk, my hands cupped around my hot chocolate and him side-eyeing me with those baby blues, I smile.

"Can I ask you something?" he asks.

"Is it if you can have a marshmallow back?"

He chokes out a laugh then shakes his head. "No. Is it…possible you can forgive me? For back then?"

"I don't know," I muse, bumping into his upper arm with my shoulder. "Were the marshmallows supposed to be a bribe?"

"Of course they were," Nic says, taking the one marshmallow still in his own drink and plopping into his mouth, tucking it into his cheek like some game of chubby bunny. "Di'it work?"

"Yeah," I say with a giggle. A freaking *giggle*. Who am I? "It might have. But only a little."

"I can accept a little," he says.

I curl my lips in and look away. I can feel my face growing hot.

Weirdly enough, I do forgive him. To what extent, I don't know, but this is a fresh start. Something new with a gorgeous, kind man far away from my hometown with bad memories and unsettling Christmases. This is Nic. And he's…different. Maybe not the Grinch after all.

After a moment, he says, "Mind if we stop by the bar on the way back to the inn? I wanna make sure our peppermint beer came in."

"Oh my god, ew."

He laughs. "The people in St. Rudolph love it, I swear."

"They must have zero taste buds," I say, scrunching my nose.

He doesn't respond for a second, only glancing from my nose back up to my eyes before saying, "You're cute when you do that." He points at my nose. "That…thing. I mean, you're cute all the time, but…"

My stomach drops right into the snow. I open my mouth to speak, but nothing comes out.

I get a small peek of his tongue between his lips, see it pull in followed by a long, soft exhalation. It's slow and… there's something else there. I can feel it worming its way into my stomach and down to my gut.

It's a look.

I know that look.

I want more of that look.

It's the look that says Nic *wants me*.

And I know I want him.

He quirks his eyebrow, and only in that moment do I realize I've been biting my own lip like some insane seductress too.

Are we just both over here seducing each other and not realizing it?

"I'm cute?" I ask.

He shakes his head, but his eyes do not leave mine. They pierce right through me.

"Can I take that back, actually?"

Oh dang, okay. You ruined it, Birdie. Great job.

"Oh?" I ask.

"Sexy." *Ohmygod.* "I meant to say you're sexy. And…" He steps forward. I let him into my space, feeling his warm chest hit mine. "Well, I'd like to show just how much I think that."

Holy Christmas spirit.

I think I might black out for a moment because I stand there with my mouth gaping open in disbelief like some fish out of water.

"If you'd like to come to the bar with me, this is," he amends.

"I could," I find myself—or at least some Birdie Mae in some universe with more confidence than me—saying, "but I could go home too."

What?!

Why am I saying that? Why are these words coming out? I know what I want, and he's handing it to me on a silver dinner platter.

But also…part of me wants to give him an out. Part of me wants to excuse him if he's just trying to be nice or something.

This is it, Nic. Take the exit. But also…don't let me go do work, Nic. Let me explore your wonderful beard and biceps. Please, for the love of Christmas.

Nic's ensuing grin is absolutely devious, and I know he's in it and so am I.

He takes a step closer, as if that's even possible.

"What do you want to do, Birdie Mae? Do you want to go home?"

I shake my head. "No."

And then Nic smiles. It breaks across his face like a kid slowly realizing they've gotten exactly the present they wanted for Christmas.

Me.

"Good," he says.

Nic holds out his hand, gesturing toward the empty hot chocolate cup still resting between my palms. I hand it to him wordlessly, and he stacks it with his, tossing it in the nearby trash can and replacing the empty space between my palms with his own hand in mine.

Nic's fingers start cupped as we walk down the sidewalk, but slowly they entwine finger by finger until we're connected, tugging each other closer and closer to the bar. I can see it farther down the street, a dull empty space on an otherwise lit street. It's the middle of the day and it isn't open. It'll just be us.

He looks over at me, a smile tugging at the edge of his mouth. Each step is being fueled by my own nerves, and each crunching footfall in the snow feels easier, like the steam is practically rolling out of my feet, making way for us to get there faster.

We bank left before the building, finding our way into an alley where we walk around back.

I want to push him against the wall right then and there.

I twist to face him right before the parallel brick walls open back up, but then my shoulder gets pushed back and I realize Nic is already two steps ahead of me.

He's pushing me up against the wall first.

I stumble back, but only for a moment before his warm gentle hands are wrapped around my waist, steadying me as I walk backward and he walks forward into me, until my back is firmly pressed against the cool brick. His hands drag their way up my sides, around the edge of my breasts, up my collar, and to my cheeks, where he holds my jaw in both of his palms and brings my mouth to his.

And, oh, it's everything.

It's heady, this kiss. It's like when my neighbors overdid their Christmas displays on their house and blew out the entire neighborhood's power. Except this time it's me. My power is sparking and getting blown out. Me and my nerves and the explosion that can't decide where it wants to go. Through my chest, down my legs, to my toes…

When his hands trail into my hair, the sensation follows. When his thumbs trace the edge of my earlobe, a shiver runs down my spine. And when his tongue finds its way between our parted lips, I'm relieved that I can finally taste him.

My hands clutch his coat. His body presses against mine and the sherpa jacket lining rubs against my exposed neck. It's soft and smells clean, just like him.

Nic presses against me harder, pushing his weight so I'm positioned against both him and the brick wall. Like I'm between a rock and…a very, very hard place.

I chance it and twist a free palm to drag down his front, over those rolling abs, clinking past his belt buckle to cup the length of him through his jeans.

Good lord, is he rocking a baseball bat in there? It feels like it goes on forever, and with one thrust of his hips against my open palm, I just know he's confirming my thoughts.

I start to stroke, wrapping my fingers around him.

He doesn't let me do it for long.

Instead, Nic grabs my wrist and raises it up to trap against the brick behind me.

"Let's go inside," he says. His voice is gruff. Definitely not like the Nic I used to know. He then leans in again to whisper into my ear, his tone sending goose bumps along my neck. "I don't want to share you with anyone else."

One hand feels up my side. It's warmer than the hot chocolate in my belly, igniting everything in me that felt like it was fading just a few days ago, brought on by the last man I thought would do it for me.

I must be staring at him with some stupid, dazed look, because when he pulls away and sees my expression, he laughs, removing his grip from my wrist and entwining his fingers in mine again.

"Come on."

Then he drags me away from the wall. It's good that he decides to do all the work in taking us where we're going, because I don't think my legs are capable of moving on their own. Not when my knees feel like jelly and his thumb is still running circles over mine. Not when he's unlocking the back door to the bar and simultaneously keeping me tucked in front of him, my ass pressed against his tight zipper. Not when I'm shoved into the darkness of the back room of the bar, his arm suddenly under my knees and back and he's literally carrying me through the back rooms and over to the main bar and placing me on the counter.

Nic places a palm against each of my knees, spreading them apart so he can take up the empty space between them. He still hasn't turned on the lights so all I can see is whatever the outside sun wants to illuminate through the dusky windows. It's not much.

"It's dark," I say dumbly.

"You're right," he agrees, leaning forward. His scent immediately overtakes me. His beard teases its way over my chest, pressing into it, placing kisses between my breasts, unclasping the buttons on my coat. Then one hand disappears far behind me, over the countertop, followed by a small *click*.

The bar brightens with cozy rainbow Christmas lights strung up on every wall, over every exposed ceiling beam, and running right below where my knees wrap over the edge of the counter.

Yes, now I can see those dimples of his—signs that he is pleased as holiday punch.

"Better," he says, running his hands along my thighs and up to my hips, gripping harder for one second as if checking if I'm even there. Then he traces them up my sides to slide my coats—one and two—off my shoulders, letting them fall behind me on the counter in one large heap. "Much better. Now I can watch you."

"Watch me what?" I ask, blinking past the glazed-over look I must have on my face at seeing how deftly his thumbs hook into my belt loops.

"I don't want to miss you enjoying yourself, Birdie Mae," he says, tucking the top button of my pants through its slit to leave only the zipper undone. "If that's okay, of course."

I swear I can hear my heartbeat in my ears. My whole head is pounding at the thought of this man. The sheer audacity of him. The confidence in his grin, his swagger as he leans against one of my open thighs, trailing his thumb up the opposite one, tracking over every ridge of my knee.

His hair, streaked with gray and bits of ginger, flops over, covering part of his eyebrows, which are raised in anticipation. He looks nothing like my other exes because while they were lovely and cute, Nicholas is a different breed of man entirely. He's all desire, awaiting the green light to devour me whole. I've never had any Santa look at me the way he looks at me now.

With hunger.

"Yes, please" is all I get out.

But it's all Nicholas needs.

My zipper is down and his hand is against my neck, cradling me as he pulls my mouth to his, gently leaning me back against the bar, covering the back of my head with his palm when it hits the countertop.

I try to hold back my gasps as he tugs my pants down.

It's cold. Real cold. And all I've got on is my simple black panties to shield me from the cool bar top. But he's feverish in his motions, ready to get down to business, and who am I to argue?

Then Nic stops tugging my pants down and simply says, "Huh."

I sit up quicker than I thought possible. My heart is picking up the pace too, and I can feel my face heating up.

"Oh my god, what what what."

I'm already in freak-out mode.

What did he see? Was it the mole on my inner thigh? Is he grossed out by the way my naked body looks on the counter? You know that weird area where the skin gets its stupid little bumpy craters near where my butt cheeks hit my saddle bags and where bathing suits never seem to forgive or forget?

But when I see him, he's not looking at my wobbly bits. He's looking down between us, where my jeans are bunched down at my feet, impeded by my boots.

"Well," he muses. "That's an easy fix."

And then my legs are lifted up—*Oh my god I don't know if I'm flexible enough for this*—and Nic steps underneath them and lowers them on the other side of him so my legs, constricted by my jeans, rest against the back of his calves.

"Okay?" he asks me with a grin.

I nod slowly and am still nodding as he presses a hand on my chest, lightly pushing me back down against the bar and bending at the waist to kiss along my inner thighs. I'm breathing heavier the closer he gets, and when he finally noses past my panty line, tracing his warm tongue against my slit, I think my heart may explode.

It doesn't have time to because in the next moment, his tongue rolls into me, lapping up my wet center, long luxurious strokes followed by short ones, concentrating at the exact spot he needs to.

This is a man with a plan.

Other Santas? What other Santas?

What other *men*?

My clit has never felt more on fire than it is right now. God, have *I* even been touching myself this deftly before? Do I even know what I like?

Because Nicholas clearly does. I know this even more concretely when I feel two fingers curl into me, dragging over my bundles of nerves over and over and over with his tongue licking and licking and licking and—

"Oh god, Nic." The words leave my mouth in a strangled mess that I hope he can decipher.

He stops for a second to mutter out a somehow sensual version of, "Mmhm?"

I pat his back. "No, don't stop. Go, go."

Teasing, he whispers, "Oh, you want me to…?"

Another stroke. Another long, languid lap of his tongue against the nerves begging to explode throughout the rest of me.

"Nic," I repeat.

"Say my name louder."

I moan, and then the man feasts.

Desperation is in every movement, growling, biting, sucking, and in no time I'm *there*.

All at once.

Just there.

And everywhere.

All the way down in Australia maybe.

And maybe even in the North Pole at this point?

God, who even knows.

I hit euphoria at the mouth of my sworn enemy, and it's never felt so right.

When I'm coming down from my high, slowly with the sensual strokes of his finger tracing my slit and him leaning his chin on my inner thigh, I sit up on my elbows and gulp back the remaining nerves.

"Thank you," he says, kissing my skin.

"Thank…what?" I say, barely blubbering out words. "No, no, thank *you*."

"Oh, well, I'm glad you liked it," he says. "Because I can't wait to do it again."

He raises his eyebrows in a knowing look. I might

just die.

He bends down to tug my pants back up my legs, making sure to plant a kiss against my knee.

"Better than Sam's lap?" he asks.

I laugh, slapping his hand away and tugging my jeans the rest of the way up.

"We're gonna talk about Santa? Right now? Really?" I ask. And the sentence rings true. Why talk about Santa when I have Nic right here? A dream man?

He grips my hips and lifts me slightly so I can shimmy my pants back over my exposed butt.

"Kidding," he says. "Good point."

But then, just to be cheeky, just to see his face heat, I say, "But he was cute, I guess."

That was apparently the very wrong thing to say. His hands may not leave my hips, but Nic takes one step away from me.

Wait, wait, come back.

"What?" he asks, his grip a bit tighter, possibly possessive. I would find it hot were he not looking like a reindeer in headlights.

"I'm joking," I say with a small laugh. "You mentioned Sam so I… It's a joke?"

"You think he's cute?"

"Oh, come on, I'm joking. Don't be the jealous type," I say. "It doesn't look good on anyone."

Nic forces a laugh, shaking his head a little bit, as if trying to shake away the thoughts in his head. I can see the battle of him possibly trying to decide whether he should say something.

But I know exactly what to do.

I take his hands in mine, tracing a line across his knuckles, and say, "I'll tell you mine if you tell me yours."

He looks up, eyes wide.

I smile, rolling my head back, and continue, "Come on, I'm feeling the spirit here."

If he doesn't talk soon, I'll just blurt out my own secret.

I date Santas.

There. Easy-peasy. The secret seems almost ridiculous now. In fact, he's gonna find it hilarious. How many people exclusively date Santas for the holidays? He'll think it's silly. And, really, it is.

"Okay, okay," Nic says. "I'll go first. But…don't laugh." He points a finger at me. I cross my heart, trying to be the good Girl Scout that I am. "It's…well, it's stupid. But, my ex-wife…she…left me for a Santa."

And then my heart flipping stops.

A record scratches somewhere in the distance, I swear.

"Wait, what."

Nic shuffles his feet under him. His rough thumbs are absentmindedly stroking over mine.

"You said you wouldn't laugh," he mutters.

"I'm not."

I would smile, but I'm still too stunned to make any motion at all.

"Okay, now tell me yours," he says, giving me the smile I should be granting him.

"Wait, no, continue," I say. "Elaborate. What happened?"

"It's…nothing," Nic says, shaking his head. He looks away, down at the button on my jeans that is now clasped closed. Or maybe he's looking at the bar top, maybe even my fingernails, but not me. He's embarrassed. "She had an affair with a mall Santa." He laughs a little at that. I just feel sick. "It sounds stupid when I say it out loud, I know. But that's why I hate Santas. Obviously not all, but…eh, I just don't trust dudes who let everyone sit in their laps."

He laughs, but I'm stunned into silence.

Nic just told me his wife left him for a Santa, and I'm about to tell him I exclusively date said Santas.

No. No no.

Is this some cruel joke?!

"Okay, your turn," he says with a nod of his head. "Yours can't be much worse, I promise."

"No, let's not underestimate me. I think it could be."

Nic laughs. "What is it?"

"I…oh god." I could just lie. That would be good. I mean, it's not like the real Santa is gonna put me on the naughty list for lying, is he?

But I can't. Not when I look up and finally see Nic's twinkling baby blue eyes shining back at me, visible relief in them. The same relief I've gotten from all these Santa apologies, like maybe he's happy I'm not judging him and his secret.

Oh buddy, don't worry, I'm too busy judging myself.

Because I'm finding myself in yet another Santa…situation. Situationship. Santa-uationship. With a dude I shouldn't even be with to begin with. Like I couldn't help myself even once.

I'm so pathetic.

So I just say it anyway.

"I…" *Pull the trigger.* "I almost exclusively date Santas, actually. Around this time of year, at least. Except I only date around this time of year, so…"

Saying it out loud is worse than I thought it'd be. I've only told this to my therapist. She cackled for a solid minute too. Nothing could be worse than that.

Nic blinks then leans back, and suddenly he barks out a laugh from the depths of his throat.

No, I take it back—Nic's reaction is worse than hers.

"Very funny," he says.

"No, I'm not trying to be funny for once, Nicholas," I say. "Sam looks like one of my exes."

"Yeah, but he's Santa."

Oh, my sweet man.

"Uh-huh," I say slowly. "And…like I said, I date Santas. Mall Santas. Parade Santas. I even had a bookstore Santa."

"You…*had* a bookstore Santa?"

He pauses, and I can tell he's mulling it over, trying to see if maybe I'm lying. He's squinting, the same way he does with all the Santas we've visited.

And it hits me…oh my god, has he been *checking*? Has he been making sure we're not seeing whichever Santa stole his wife? The realization settles in my gut, and I feel even more sick. He put himself through that just to support my dumb apology tour, and for what? To give fake apologies to my non-exes who I used for my own screwed-up coping mechanism?

Of course he thinks I'm lying. It's a ridiculous truth.

"Is that why you like me?" he asks. "Is this some type of kink or…"

"No!" I practically yell, at least it feels that way. He even jumps a bit. "No. I mean, well, yes and no. It's complicated. I mean, no, not really. You're…" I can't find the words. I can feel the heat in my cheeks rising, the nerves throughout my chest spreading up and over my neck, radiating down into the pit of me, and not good nerves. It's not the kind that was paired with a mind-blowing orgasm he just gave me.

"I'm what?" he asks.

"I don't know," I say. "You're not who I expected."

He takes a step back, shaking his head, and then his hands leave my hips.

"I'm just another Santa to you, aren't I? Another notch in your weird reindeer reins or something."

"That's a good analogy, but no. No, I promise. I don't date Santas because…they're hot or anything. I mean, not the holly jolly beer gut men, you know? It's men my age. Men who are temporary." His face falls, and I shake my head. "I mean, I don't generally date older men with the white beards, you know? Well, I did that one time, but that's beside the point. It…am I making any sense here?"

I'm blabbing, and he's quiet. So eerily quiet.

"I can't," Nic finally says, and that's when I see the hurt in his eyes. The blues have a twinkle, but…I don't know if it's the same type of twinkle I've been seeing up to now. I think it might be a tear, and god if that doesn't put the coal right in your stocking.

"Can't what?" I ask, almost a whisper.

"I just…I can't be another Santa to someone. I can't… risk being left for another Santa either."

"That…that isn't what this is." I lean forward and whisper, "Also, this is the weirdest conversation."

"Yeah, well, trust me, I've had weirder," he says before letting out a long, exasperated sigh. "Like when my wife left me for a Santa. That was pretty freaking weird."

Right.

"Nic…I'm so sorry. I… You aren't and haven't been the reason my Christmases suck." It feels right to say because he isn't. My Christmases have been comprised of horrible coincidences, but it's not him. It couldn't be this nice guy. It's all coming out wrong, but I can't stop now. "You're you. You're…Nicholas, the cool guy. Not the… sucky Krampus dude, and not some random Santa either."

He reaches his hand up to squeeze the bridge of his nose.

"I'll be honest, Birdie Mae. I don't really wanna get into this right now."

"But I'm supposed to leave tomorrow," I say, and just as the meek words leave my mouth, the quiet reality settles in my mind.

I might be leaving tomorrow. And it feels wrong. I didn't realize how much I didn't want to leave, and yet here I am, reaching out to the man I believed was my own personal Grinch and wanting nothing more than to be hand-in-hand with him singing around the Christmas tree in the square with the rest of Whoville.

"I just... Let me think," he says. "For tonight, at least. I...I can call you at the inn before you leave."

"Nic..." I'm pleading, and ugh it sounds so pathetic, but I feel pathetic. It's begging my mom to see Santa all over again. It's begging her to drive to the hospital faster again. It's every Christmas wish that never came true.

"I'm sorry, Birdie Mae. I really am," Nic says. "I just need to think."

So, I hop off the counter, tug on my coats—one and two—then make my way through the back door.

And when I step outside, it's snowing again.

CHAPTER *eight*

I saw Mommy ki—

"I'm gonna miss Christmas, Anne. There're no flights out today, and tomorrow's are up in the air too. Well…not *in the air*. Well, who knows."

"Beem."

"I'll be home for you. For her," I continue. "After Christmas."

"You've never been a huge fan of Christmas with Momma, Birdie," Anne says. "I get it." Her voice is low, exhausted, and I can feel the twitches in my fingers stretching up my arms. I feel too big for my body, like my nerves are literally stretching me thin.

"Anne, this isn't on purpose," I plead, but somehow it feels like a lie. Didn't I want to stay? Didn't I want to avoid the mess of the holidays this year?

"No, I get it," Anne says. "I do. And I've checked the flights too. You're right."

I pause. "You didn't believe me…?"

She doesn't answer my question.

"I understand, I do," she says. "But…this has gotta stop. You can't keep blaming her."

My heart freezes.

"What?"

"You do blame her," she says. "I know you do. You were so young. But just find it in your heart to forgive her."

I pull my knees up to my chest, peering out the window that looks painted white by all the snow. I can barely make out our broken-down fort from two days ago.

"I do forgive her." I breathe out. "She didn't do anything wrong. I know. It's just…she doesn't remember him except for now. And it's…"

"It's a lot. I'm telling you, Beem, I get it." Anne is tired. I can tell. She has the same tone she had with me when I was a kid, when I first yelled at Mom in the hospital the night Dad died. "But, it's life. Sometimes that's life. Sometimes it isn't some make-believe wonderland with sexy Santa books and fake Santas." I lean back on my bedpost, the weight of her words settling uneasy on me like a bruise. "Come home, Beem. Dad dying was hard. Mom's dementia is hard. This breakup is hard. But you can't keep putting yourself through the ringer for it all."

And then it all comes crashing down on me.

It's not Nic's so-called curse or my mom. It's me.

Oh my Santa, *I'm* the worst. To my mom year after year. To Nic. To myself.

It's been twenty years since The Curse, but The Curse was me. Me not coping. Me not dealing appropriately.

"I gotta go," I say, pulling back the covers. The cold has never felt more cleansing. "I'll see you tomorrow."

"Will you?"

"I promised you I'd be home for Christmas," I say. "I'll find a way to be home. And Anne?"

"Yeah?"

"I'm sorry."

———

I know where I'm headed.

I don't stop to shower. I don't stop for breakfast—okay, maybe a quick to-go cup of coffee from the inn common room—but I barrel down the sidewalks with my boots crunching over the new piles of snow with only one destination in mind: the final Santa.

Last stop. End of the line.

The true apology. It's important that I say what needs to be said. It's gonna hurt like Rudolph being bullied in the reindeer games, but I have to do it. And it will only be the start, a trial run before the real deal.

I don't glance at the bookstore as I walk by. I definitely don't look up at my illustrated Santas rooting me on through the window. I keep walking until I reach the final Santa.

I get to the small toy store at the opposite end of the downtown area. It's small and cozy like most of the stores here, but it only takes one cursory glance to see that it's unique. There are rare toys on the shelves that I haven't seen in years, like some blast from the past. Vintage, first edition items. I feel transported back to 1999.

It's a perfect setting for the perfect apology.

Time to Jingle Bell *Rock*.

It's almost ten in the morning. They're only just opening and the lone elf staff member is yawning, but just beside him, hands in his lap, is him.

The final Santa.

I walk to the line, stopping just behind the only other person. I inhale deeply and try to keep a level head. I probably look like someone who has been imbibing too much holiday rum, but I'm focused. Then the boy in front turns to face me and it's Cooper. His eyes are wide, and his bottom lip sticks out slightly.

"You go first," Cooper says, stepping aside.

I shake my head quickly, still trying to maintain my zen.

"No, you were here first," I say.

Cooper blows out a breath of air, putting his hands on his hips like he means business.

"Listen, if you're an adult with your own money and you *still* need to talk to Santa, you definitely need him more than me."

My face falls.

"How was that both kind and rude all at once?" I ask.

"Sometimes you just need tough love."

I scrunch my lips to the side and my eyes burn.

Oh god, is this kid gonna make me cry?

No, instead, I bend down to his level and ask, "What do you want for Christmas, Cooper?"

"A snowball cannon to win the snowball fight next year."

I laugh. "Aw, don't you want something less destructive like gloves or socks?"

"Maybe this is why you guys lost."

I straighten back up to my full height. "Ugh, never mind, you're the worst."

Cooper smiles, and I give him a small high five before walking up toward the throne where my salvation awaits.

Final Santa is on his game, I can tell. His eyes are not crystalline baby blues like Nic's, but boy I don't know if I've ever seen a more picturesque children's book Santa in my life. I don't think a single thing about him is fake. Not the belly that is likely full of warm cookies, not the cheeks that seem genuinely flushed instead of rouged (I can even spot the itty bitty spider veins winding up the side of his nose), and definitely not that smile beaming back at me.

He adores this gig and, more than that, I know I've chosen the right Santa for last.

"First child of Christmas Eve," he says with a smile.

Ah, dude even has jokes.

I puff out a breath of air. "And boy do I have a zinger for you, so listen up, pal. First, that kid—yeah that one—wants a snowball cannon. Can you do that for him?"

"Done."

"Good." I make a mental note to search for one before I leave anyway because fake Santas are still fake Santas, no matter how convincing. "And as for me, for Christmas, I want to do an apology. Right now. A real one. A good one. This is my confession, and you are my priest."

Without even skipping a beat, he says, "I'm all ears."

Oh, he's good.

It almost knocks me off balance, but I keep trucking. I'm on a mission.

"I…want to apologize for me."

"For you?"

"Yes. For how I've been. How I've acted. For blaming my mom for something that wasn't her fault. For…blaming my bad Christmases on some make-believe curse created in my head. I've gotta get a grip. It's nobody's fault Christmas sucks sometimes. Not Mom's. Heck, it's not even Saint Nicholas's fault."

He chortles a little laugh. It's cute.

"Me?" he asks.

"Oh, no, not you," I say with a wave of my hand and a mirroring laugh. "The other Nic. My Nic."

My Nic. It feels weirdly right.

Let's forget the part where we totally didn't have a conversation about our relationship, situationship, or whatever it is. He's mine, and he needs to know it.

"Well," Fake Santa says with a deep intake of air, "that's a lot to hold in on Christmas Eve."

I smile down at him. "That's why I'm letting it all out. I wanted to make sure it sounded good before I started calling people and whatnot."

"I'm happy for you." Final Santa gives a slight nod. "Good to take ownership."

"Thank you. I think I feel the Christmas spirit again." His hand drifts a bit lower down my back, and I lift an eyebrow. "Not like that, buddy. Don't ruin this."

He laughs. "Oh ho ho no, my apologies. I'm a bit tired. Not trying to…that. Not."

I believe him. He does look a little tired. Plus, I know he wouldn't dare touch my bottom because the real Santa doesn't do that, and if there was a real Santa, he'd be it. Hands down.

And I'm not at all attracted to him.

Imagine that.

"Ready to tackle Christmas Eve?" he asks me.

"Yes," I say. "I think so. Off to apologize to the man I like."

And I do. I like him. Too much. That ol' Saint Nick.

"Then go spread the Christmas spirit."

"I will, Santa. I will."

I boop his nose because it somehow seems like the right thing to do in that moment then hop off his lap. Cooper gives me a little thumbs-up from the line. I give him one back.

As I turn toward the exit, I almost bump into the figure in front of me. I'm glad I don't, because right there, like a

Christmas miracle—no, *the* Christmas miracle—is the one man I want to apologize to.

"Nicholas," I say breathlessly.

He looks just as breathless as me. I don't know if he ran here, but his chest is rising and falling quickly, and he has that little stray strand of hair flopping in front. Yet, even so, he's smiling.

"You didn't answer the inn's phone," Nic says. "I thought maybe you left."

"I didn't."

"Yes, I can see that. Somehow I knew I'd find you here."

Then he winks. And it's so gosh darn adorable.

I roll my eyes with a smile, edging closer to him like a magnet drawn to its equal and opposite counterpart. "I was coming to you next, I promise. I had to get my thoughts together, but…you know what, I can say this somewhere else. We should talk."

"I agree. We should…"

He looks past me and his face falls. First his gorgeous smile, followed by his eyebrows, and somehow even the twinkle in those baby blues disappears. His expression is completely blank. Ashen. All the color lost so that his skin is paler than his beard.

I almost wonder if he sees another incoming snowball, until…

"You son of a bitch," Nic says.

"What?" I squeak, turning to follow his line of sight to Final Santa, whose shocked expression is an exact—yet less symmetrical and manly—mirror of Nic's. Except for when his lip curls up. And then he looks downright menacing.

"Harold, I was told you left town," Nic continues. "I knew you didn't. I knew…"

What in the sugar plum fairies is this?

"Nicholas!" I hold out my hand to stop him because suddenly he's attempting to storm past me. "Nic, what are you doing?"

But I know exactly what he's doing. My brain is connecting the dots before the rest of me can react, including my words.

"Stop!" I finally get out, twisting to follow him up the stairs, reaching out for his arm and tugging on the bicep. It's hard as a rock under my touch, and it takes everything in me to not get turned on by this fact.

No, focus. He's picking a fight with Santa. Let's not get aroused right now.

"You promised you'd leave town," Nic says through gritted teeth.

Final Santa grins. "No, I said I wasn't working the square this year."

The square. The event. Last Christmas…

This fake Santa is the Santa his wife left him for.

Oh holy night.

"Liar," Nic says. "You promised…"

"And your wife promised you vows, but that didn't work out either, did it?"

I gasp. Cooper gasps. The helper elf gasps. I think even the plastic reindeer gasp.

"That's not very Santa of you," I mutter.

Final Santa—freaking *Harold*—narrows his eyes. "I'm sorry, did I ruin Christmas for you?"

Yes. Yes he freaking did! Not Momma. Not Nicholas. But freaking *Harold*.

I'm much more okay with blaming the horribleness of Christmas past on Harold.

"I wasted my last apology on you!" I say with a pointed finger. And then suddenly it's Nic holding *me* back as I wiggle in his tight grip. "Let me go, Nic! My mental breakthrough now means nothing if he was the one to listen!"

"No," Nic says, his mouth a thin line. "You know what?"

I take a deep inhalation. "What?"

"He's not even worth it, Birdie Mae."

Even in my time of anger, the sound of my name on his lips sends my soul flying back to Earth and through his grasp to both our hearts.

"He's not?"

"No. That sack of human garbage is not worth it," Nic repeats, keeping a harsh glare on Harold, as if making sure the words hit him like a dart to the soul. "Trust me on that."

I turn around to look at Nic, taking in his eyes, his cheeks, his beautiful lips.

"You sure? Because I'm riled up and ready to go." I throw a mock punch.

He chuckles. "Yeah, I'm sure." Then he leans in, pressing a small kiss on my forehead, and I sigh, melting into it. "Come on," he says. "Let's go."

I'm looking at him and he's looking at me and all I want is to just kiss his face and hug him and protect him from the false Santa that is beside us, the true Grinch who stole Christmas.

Am I being cheesy? I'm being cheesy.

But when else should you be cheesy other than during Christmas, huh?

And then suddenly there are more gasps, and they're not coming from me or Nic. It's Cooper, who is pulling on Harold's beard and saying, "You're a faker! You're a big old fake phony! And you hurt Mr. Nicholas!"

"Get off, kid," he says, shoving Cooper. Cooper falls to the ground. It's not rough, but it's enough to make my head hurt from anger. And Cooper is already tearing up, his little lip wobbling.

The next thing I know, Nic is barreling up the red carpet, directly toward Harold, and he socks him right in that red, spider-veined nose.

I hope he broke it.

CHAPTER *nine*

"OUCH, OUCH, OUCH."

"Don't be a big ol' baby," I mutter, giving a small peck to the side of his beard as I press a bag of frozen peas to the other cheek.

Four exchanged punches, three witnesses, two fist bumps from Cooper, and one police report later, we're back at Nic's apartment above the bookstore. All we're missing is a partridge in a pear tree.

I sit on his comfy leather couch across from him, planting the occasional kiss on his bruising cheek.

"You think I can take the night off?" he asks.

"And where would people get their Christmas Eve presents?"

"I'm not Santa, Birdie Mae."

The comment should sting, but it doesn't. Because for once, I don't mean it.

"I know. I meant peppermint beer." I lower the peas, looking him in the eye with a deep inhalation and an equally exhausted exhalation. "You know I'm not into you because you look like Santa, right?"

"You're into me?"

We exchange small smiles, his with a dimple and a

slight wince at the pain. I gently place the peas back on the ever-growing purple cheek welt.

He finally clears his throat and pulls back as I lower the peas between us.

"I have some things I'd like to say, if that's alright."

I smile. "Okay, go for it."

He shrugs. "More like confessions."

"Call me Father Birdie. Well, actually, no don't. That sounds wrong. Is that wrong?"

He chuckles, winces and brings his hand to his cheek, and then sighs.

"I'm sorry for getting defensive about the whole Santa thing," he says. "It's not my place to judge why you do what you do. And I know it's no reflection on me."

"I promise my reasons for dating Santas aren't weird, I swear." *Well, kinda*, I think after. When I purse my lips to the side, I think he reads my mind, because he laughs again.

"Ah, stop making me smile. You do that, you know? All the time. You...you have this light about you."

"Light?"

"Shush, I'm being corny." I bite my lip, and he continues. "You changed my life twenty years ago. I mean it when I say that. I was about to be eighteen. All I had was the system throwing me around my whole life, and I was working some dumb part-time job just to stay out of trouble. Then you came along, some spunky little girl excited about the idea of Christmas. Eleven and still believing in Santa Claus."

"Not exactly proud of that."

"It was endearing. I believe, as dumb as it is, that you were some holiday miracle like they always talk about."

"Oh come on."

He shakes his head with a smile on his face that seems

so genuine and kind, but then again, everything about Nicholas is genuine and kind.

"No, that's how I saw it," he continues. "A sign. Once I turned eighteen, I turned my life around. I moved as far away as I could. Picked a random spot on a map and made a fresh start here. Met my ex-wife, and for a while I was happy. And I loved Christmases. I mean, just absolutely embraced the whole thing. I helped coordinate the Eve Eve parade, set up the peppermint beer craze, started the tradition of all those snowball fights…"

"Clearly," I snort.

"Hey," he warns with a grin, then his face falls. "And then…and then she left me." I feel my chest split at the sudden change, the man who was so excited now just defeated. "I've run through the possible reasons a billion times, but there's no point in fooling myself. I know what happened. Everything started when I said I wanted kids and she didn't. I didn't push it, but it opened a door we couldn't close." His lip twitches, like he's trying to smile but can't bring himself to. "So then…when it all happened, I got in a huge fight in the square with… freaking Harold."

"Freaking Harold," I echo.

"I stopped volunteering at Christmas. I moved in here. Kinda secluded myself from everything but the bar. And I'm…sorry for putting my burdens on you when it's not your fault I'm bitter about Santas."

"I think we've both played some version of the blame game," I admit. "It's funny…you're the last stop on my apology tour," I mutter, curling my legs in.

"Am I?" he asks, placing his hand lightly on my knee. It's such a natural gesture, like it was meant to belong there.

"Yeah," I say. "I…blamed a lot of my Christmas junk

on you. Honestly, for my entire life, like you're some ghost of Christmas past."

He eyebrows scrunch in, forming a cute line on his forehead.

"And what happened, Birdie Mae? What did I do?"

Our eyes catch, and I swallow down my pride.

"You said I'd hate Christmas. That's it. That's all. It's dumb when I think about it, really, but after that...it seemed like everything changed," I say. "Well, seemed that way because it did. My dad...he...passed away on that night we met when I was a kid. Freak car accident. He was getting extra presents, which is just..." I laugh a little, but it feels bittersweet. "It's just something he would do. And my mom well...my mom... Anyway, I've always sorta... blamed you."

Nic doesn't say anything, but I'm not even sure what I'd want him to say at this point, or if he even should talk. Maybe he knows that because he leans in to press his forehead to mine, closing his eyes. I close mine too, feeling his slow steady breaths against my own.

After a moment, he pulls away, planting a chaste kiss right at my hairline as he whispers, "I'm sorry for your loss, Birdie Mae."

The tone is low and deep and full of all the comforts that should come with an apology. I've never had anyone respond with that much weight before, and I know he means every syllable of it.

"Thank you."

"And your mom?" he asks.

"My mom was late to the hospital. I mean, she couldn't have helped Christmas traffic, but he was gone by the time we got there. I'd never fought with her before then, but after that it was all I could do. It wasn't her fault. I know that now...but she doesn't. To her, he's still alive every

Christmas. It's like every holiday season, we're right back at our house in '99 and she's wondering where he is. She didn't start to go…well, her memory didn't start to go until a few years back, early onset and all, but of course that's the one nightmare we can't move past even when she doesn't remember much. And sometimes it's hard to handle."

I hate that I can see my pain reflected back at me in his gaze. I hate that I can feel it in my own soul after it having lain dormant for years.

"Every year since then, I've hated Christmas," I continue. "Just like you said I would."

"So you thought I cursed you."

"Yeah."

"If you hate Christmas, what's with the Santas then?"

I sigh, smiling at the ridiculousness despite myself. It prompts Nic to smile too, which makes my heart feel warm, if that's even a thing.

"Santa was always the one piece of the puzzle that made things okay. He was just the happy guy having a good time no matter what happened. The 'spirit' of Christmas. He had the one thing I think I lost." I laugh, shaking my head. "God, it's so cheesy and dumb, and leave it to a writer to make things more meaningful than they need to be."

I'm babbling, I know, but Nicholas bends his head down, tracing a finger along the outside of my thumb, down my wrist, and to my elbow, pulling it in so my arms wrap around his middle. I scoot forward on the couch, letting myself settle into his lap. My other hand picks up the bag of peas from the couch and drops it to the ground beside us as his hand reaches behind my neck to lay my head against his chest.

We're hugging. It's warm and comfortable. I'm

breathing in his scent of fresh holiday pine and warm peppermint, letting the fibers of his flannel tickle my cheek.

We're in that position for a while. I think I'm nuzzling him at one point, but I don't care. I don't think he does either. His hands entwine below my spine, a thumb hooking into one of my empty belt loops.

My own hands eventually make their way to his hair, letting his thick locks slide over and through my fingertips. He lets out a low moan, but it isn't erotic. Well, okay, it is a little, but mostly it's peaceful. He's melting into my shoulder just as I'm letting myself relax into his chest.

A perfect fit.

"I have a gift for you," Nic mutters against my neck after who knows how long. The broken silence causes me to finally pull away. "Don't go anywhere," he says, the grin forming at the edge of his lips, tugging at a lone dimple under his beard. He plants a small kiss on the tip of my nose, reaching his hands underneath my legs to gently lift me off him.

Once I'm slid to the side enough, he's up and across the room, grabbing something out of his wardrobe and twisting on the spot with whatever this gift is hidden behind his back.

"It's a restraining order, isn't it?" I ask.

"Caught me."

He takes more steps toward me. His arms look really nice pulled back like that. His chest fills his whole shirt. It's mouth-watering.

"No, I take it back. Definitely something sexy," I say on impulse, my face reddening at the idea and the fact that I just said that out loud.

He quirks up an eyebrow, a small lift of his lips following. I could die a happy woman under that stare.

"Maybe later," he growls. "But first…"

And then he pulls out the box from behind him, and it's…

"A Furby," I say. But the words don't come out; they're only mouthed through the high-pitched garble of sounds that could possibly make out the name.

"Your very own," he says, placing it in my hands.

It's the purple one. The one with the spots.

"How did you get this?"

"The toy store downtown has all sorts of unique nostalgia toys," he says. "The second you seemed like you didn't get one, I went and asked if they had any. Seems like their stock is better than most stores in the 90s."

"You couldn't get one anywhere," I say. "Didn't this one spy on the White House at one point? Ah, who knows, who cares."

It's fluffy and bug-eyed and the beak is all shiny, pristine from years in the packaging. It's perfect.

I don't even have to say it. He knows how much this means to me. But I say it anyway.

"I can't believe you did this," I say. "I mean, you got me a toy."

"Well, not a sexy kind of toy, but if I had known…"

I look up at him, and he throws me a quick wink. It's so subtle but so powerful. It melts me to my icy core.

Nic plops back down on the couch, not even being shy about how quickly he leans in to kiss my neck, up the column of my throat, and across my jaw.

"You're looking like you want to give me a different kind of toy now," I say.

"You won't need one," he growls.

"Oh." I extend my arm out to feel over to the coffee table where I set the packaged Furby down.

Nic hums against my skin. The sound radiates through

my chest so much it's like my now Furby-less hand can't help but use the bottled energy to reach down and stroke the edge of his jeans. I lift his shirt as he hovers over me, and my knuckles graze the bit of hair just below his navel, trailing down into the band of his boxers.

His nose brushes over my cheek to my ear. I love feeling his weight on me, the pine scent of him drifting over me, but I want something else more. I want him.

I push his chest, shifting to sit on my knees and rising up to ease him backward so I fall on top of him. I place my hands on either side of his torso, bending down to bite his earlobe.

The low moan from his throat echoes throughout the apartment as his hands find my hips, using his strength to reposition me so I straddle right over him. I lower down, grinding against him.

I lick my lips and Nic lets out a borderline shaky exhalation as he watches me do it. One hand leaves my hip to tuck a strand of my loose hair behind my ear. I've seen movie after movie of guys doing that, and it doesn't even remotely rival the real thing. With one gentle tug at the end of my strand, I'm coaxed back down to him where our mouths finally meet once more—like old friends.

Dirty, nasty, desperate ones.

One second his lips are caressing mine, opening and closing, licking the edges to request entry. It's kind, sweet, polite. Then the next second it's wanting. Greedy. My tongue makes first contact this time, desperate to taste every bit of him. I want the bite of his peppermint, the sting of his fingers as they grip my hip harder, the rumble of his groan in my mouth as I fist a lock of his thick hair.

Nic's arms wrap around me and I'm lifted again. I steady myself by gripping his biceps, thick and bulging and rock hard as he drops his feet to the floor in front of the couch, sitting forward and placing me down to straddle him.

His hands trail the edge of my shirt, snaking under the hem, thumbing where the curve of my breast meets my ribs. He's teasing me, kissing the tip of my other breast, his breath hot even through the two layers of fabric.

I rub him through his jeans, stroking the length of him, wondering where the end even is. He's long; I can already feel that, and just the thought of him inside me has me panting.

I start to undo his buckle the moment he lifts my shirt the rest of the way, tugging it over my head and tossing it to the floor. He rubs a thumb over my exposed nipple, hardening them more than they already were, and places his mouth over it.

His tongue is borderline magical, I swear. He gives my nipple a quick nip, and I let out a totally inhuman moan.

I release his buckle, the clinks of the metal spurring me forward, the teeth of his zipper ripping downward under my thumb, sending sparks across my chest. Though maybe that's just his second bite to my nipple.

Nic lifts his hips so I can slide down his jeans and boxer briefs past his knees. I don't hesitate to look down as his erection springs free. It catches on the last bit of the boxers, and boy oh boy. If I thought he was big before, I was wrong. He has a small, trimmed tuft of hair at the base, trailing up to a veiny shaft and bright red head.

I don't want to wait.

As if reading my mind, he pulls out the drawer of his side table to grab a silver wrapper. He rips it with his straight, beautiful teeth before rolling it over himself. For a second, I wonder if it'll cover it all, but I remember in college there was a sex ed demonstration where the lady put her whole leg in one of these, so I guess if she can fit that in then he just might be able to fit it over himself.

I'm too busy staring and am startled when I feel his palm run over my cheek.

"Hey, is this alright?" he asks.

"Oh, don't worry about me," I say with wide eyes. "Unless you think you'll split me in half with that thing, in which case, eh, maybe worry a bit."

He barks out a laugh. The nice one that I adore.

"Off with the pants," he demands. I am more than happy to oblige.

I hop off his lap, kicking off my boots—because I learned my lesson last time—then tugging my pants the rest of the way over my feet.

"Not getting stuck this time," I say, one finger raised in declaration.

He tilts his head to the side. "Aw, I kinda liked having you tied up in some way."

My chest burns with anticipation.

I look around the room, and just above him, I see Christmas lights. He follows my gaze up and grins.

"Oh, Birdie Mae…are you having ideas?"

"Maybe?"

"Get that naked ass over here."

I look down and cringe. I'm standing in front of him completely naked, and I hadn't even fully registered that until now. I rush to him, straddling his legs once more. He immediately kisses my chest, my neck, my cheek, and finally my lips, taking my chin between his forefinger and thumb.

"You're so beautiful," he whispers against my lips.

"So…the uh…" I nod my head up to the lights strung on the wall.

He raises an eyebrow. A single eyebrow that makes my stomach flip.

"Don't threaten me with a good time," Nic says through a laugh, licking a line between my breasts. He absentmindedly reaches a hand up behind him, tugging down the Christmas lights tacked to his wall. A clatter of pins fall to the hardwood. "Hands behind your back."

I'm much too eager to please because I put my hands behind me, continuing to grind myself against his length as he peers over my shoulder to knot my wrists together with a rainbow of Christmas lights. At his final jerk to secure the knot in place, I can't help but gasp.

One finger drags up my arm and to my neck, where he leans forward to plant one small kiss after another before grabbing my hips with both paws and gliding me up his length.

I bend down to kiss him one last time, lingering in the moment before spreading my thighs wider and letting him notch at my entrance.

In my doing so, my feet knock the coffee table, and I hear a very low, odd whine.

Oh God my wrists are tied and someone broke in.

That's my first thought.

But then we both turn to look behind me.

It's the Furby, on the ground, somehow making noises.

I knew not to trust it.

"Do you think it'll watch us?" I ask, turning back to Nic.

He raises one dirty eyebrow, and the simple, seductive gesture hooks around my gut and pulls me closer.

"Oh, I sure hope it does, Birdie Mae."

My chest burns for him.

"You're a naughty man."

"No, I think you're the one who will make the naughty list this year," he says.

I lower myself down on his cock and slide him in. It's easier than I thought and even easier when his thumb goes to rub circles over my clit. I'm probably only halfway down —if that—but then he grips my hips and raises me up then back down, letting us find our rhythm, letting me adjust around him.

And then we're moving.

His head is hanging over the back of the couch, watching me through his thick, beautiful eyelashes as I ride him with the help of his guiding hands. His eyes are a crystal-clear star in the dusk of night, and I'm following him home.

It only makes me take more of him.

Over and over, pounding harder and harder, his hands gripping my hips to guide me. The sounds of our bodies echo throughout the room. The moans leaving my mouth and the grunts from his synchronize together in some holiday symphony. It blends with the bells outside, the whistle of the Christmas Eve wind, and the joy of holiday fervor coming from holiday shoppers down on the sidewalk.

Eventually he leans forward and grips the knot of lights behind me, letting my back bow into him. His tongue meets my nipple, and a rush of sensation travels down to my stomach.

It's euphoric.

I orgasm before he does, and I think my desperate moan of his name is what does him in, but not before he licks at my breasts like a man devouring a candy cane, sending me into a second one.

Nic lets out a breathy grunt of "Damn, Birdie Mae" that sends shivers over my whole body.

And then I collapse on top of him.

We lie there breathing heavy. He runs a palm over my back, and I kiss the smattering of curled hair on his chest. After a moment, he unties the rope of lights at my wrists, and with my hands now free, I entwine them through his.

"Where have you been my whole life?" he asks me, and the words settle deep in my soul because I don't know a way to tell him I've been wondering the same thing.

"Dating the wrong people, that's where."

He chuckles, burying his face in my neck and planting a deep kiss at my pulse.

His head falls back and he groans. "Ugh, I've gotta go serve peppermint beer with a crooked nose and a purple cheek."

"You know, that was one impressive punch you threw," I say.

Nic laughs again.

"I'll punch another guy if it'll get you wet like that again."

"It was the Furby."

"Naughty girl."

We both laugh and he leans back, sighing.

But we don't say anything because there's nothing to be said. There's just the silence of the room, our own little private snow globe, encased in Christmas joy.

"Well, I've gotta finish a book," I say. "So I'll go with you to the bar and write it there if you like. I'll even make it a sexy bartender Santa."

He leans up to kiss the tip of my nose, and I swear I swoon.

"I'd like nothing more."

CHAPTER ten

Nic makes us bacon and eggs at his place after he closes up the bar. It's too late for dinner and too early for breakfast, but who cares?

He reaches for my hand while he's scrambling the eggs, bringing the back of it up to his lips, tracing each knuckle with a whisker of his beard.

It's every bit of Christmas magic tied up into one motion.

After the food is made, we sit across from each other at his breakfast nook. It's dark in the apartment, only lit by the colored, taboo Christmas lights I strung up again to decorate the fireplace and kitchen cabinets.

Though I'm enjoying my eggs—seriously, what spices did he put in here?—I look up and find him staring at me, biting his lip in thought.

"You look tired," he says.

"Rude," I say with a smile. "You're one to talk."

"No, no, you look stressed. I expected you to catch a plane by now."

My face falls.

"If I didn't know any better, I'd think you read my mind," I say.

"No, I just saw the alert on your phone," he responds with a cocky grin. His smile is unreadable, but if I had to guess, it might look more on the sad side than happy.

I bought a flight after I finished writing my book. It's why I gathered my stuff from the inn and brought it here as he closed up the bar. I intend to call a ride soon that will drive me three hours to an airport with no snow that actually has working flights leaving to Georgia.

I hadn't told Nic yet.

"I want to stay," I say. "I do, but I promised my sister I'd get home."

"I know, and you should go. It's the right thing to do," he says.

"I couldn't *not* buy the ticket," I continue, as if needing to justify it. But when he smiles, full on with dimples and all, I can tell I don't need to. I continue anyway. "I guess I almost thought I'd get out of it this year, but I can't. I need to be home for Anne. For my mom."

He laughs. "Why does this feel like an apology, Birdie Mae? Go. Be with your family." And there's not a hint of disdain in his voice. No sign at all. If anything, his little dimpled grin says he's disappointed I haven't left already.

At least I think that's what it says.

But I'm not ready to leave him yet, and maybe that's why he's smiling. He knows I'm procrastinating, and it's not just his bacon and eggs or his brilliant tongue that just a few hours ago was swiping across every inch of me with the promise of more if I asked. It's him, the Grinch who stole my heart.

"Do you... You wouldn't wanna spend time with me and my family at Christmas, would you?" I ask. "I know that's a lot, but...well..."

My words fade, but his smile deepens. Both dimples this time. Double score. Touchdown. Goal. Some other sports analogy that would make me feel like I won the World Cup.

And there's that twinkle in his eye shining right back as well.

"Actually, I'd be honored, Birdie Mae."

———

Christmas Day, 10:00am

I saw Mommy kissing Santa Claus, underneath the mistletoe last night. She didn't see me—

My alarm goes off just enough to wake me up, but it's not me who shuts it off. It's Nic. My Nic. The man whose sweater is currently collecting my drool.

I jolt upright, trying to assess my surroundings. Where am I? I'm in a car. Outside the window, there's no snow. We're in a suburban neighborhood. Ah, one I know all too well.

"How long have I been out?" I ask him.

"Thirty minutes, give or take a few."

I rub a palm over my eyes. "I should have slept on the plane."

Nic chuckles, wrapping an arm over my shoulder.

"You were too busy corralling everyone into singing *Jingle Bells*."

My eyes widen. "I thought that was a hallucination."

He barks out a laugh. "Oh, I hope it wasn't."

I lightly swat his shoulder, not enough for it to matter.

He probably doesn't feel my tiny palm on those big, muscled biceps of his anyway.

My phone buzzes in my lap, and I know who it is before I even see the caller ID.

I unlock it with a smile.

"Listen, it's okay that you didn't make it," Anne says without me even giving a greeting.

"I promised I would," I say.

I share a knowing look with Nic, who mouths, "Your sister?"

I nod.

"That's cute, but it's Christmas and you're not here, Beem." She lets out a weak, slightly sad laugh, like it's bubbling up within her.

"No, no, *you're* cute, lovely sister of mine," I say. "I promised I'd be there on Christmas, so I will be."

"You don't know that."

I do know that because we're getting out of the car at the curb. Because Nic is getting our suitcases out of the trunk and because we're rolling them up the driveway.

Anne's driveway.

It doesn't look like St. Rudolph here. There's no subtle jingle bell background soundtrack and no quaint bookstores. There's no old town aesthetic with crossing wooden beams or gas lamps. Just a two-story suburban brick house in a long line of similar designs. Some have mown grass. Others have deflated Christmas decorations. The rest just have a hedge or two.

It's ordinary. All of it.

And yet, this is home to me. It may not be *my* house, but it's where my heart is.

Nic looks down at me, taking my hand in his and giving it a squeeze as he kisses my forehead.

"You're cute, Anne."

"How can I be cute?" Anne asks, exasperated. "You don't even know how I'm dressed."

"I'm imagining matching pajamas with the family with your hair in a wild bun?"

"We do that every year."

"Yes, but I'll find out soon if I'm right," I say into the phone. "Like, now-ish."

"Now?" Anne says. "Come on, be serious."

"I am."

"No, Birdie. We're about to open presents and head to see Momma, and if—"

"Seriously," I say. "I'm here."

Nic rings the doorbell, and I can hear the reverb on her end of the line as well.

There are some tiny footsteps, and the handle turns in two seconds flat. The door opens and there is my nephew, in snowman pajamas, his hair messy and carefree. His tooth wiggles out front. Soon it'll be gone, and he'll look just like Cooper. Behind him is my niece in pink snowman pajamas with her wild doe eyes as if she can't believe I'm in front of her.

"Aunt Beem!" she yells.

They both attack my legs with a hug.

And then, in the hallway beyond, there's Anne, in matching pajamas as I guessed, her hand still plastered to the phone, looking me up and down as if she can't believe I'm standing right here right now. I guess I really can't either.

Her eyes drift to Nicholas, which causes them to practically bulge out of her head.

Yeah, I know the feeling, sis.

"If you found another Santa, so help me..."

"I'm the best one, trust me," Nic says with a wink that nearly knocks me off my feet and definitely knocks my sister over. That or her socks slip on the hardwood floor.

"Christ!"

"...mas."

"Beem!"

Nic and I both reach over her kids and grab her elbow to steady her.

"I told you not to buy the fuzzy ones," I say.

"Mae-bae!"

My brother-in-law, Brian, calls my nickname from the banister, running down in his own wacky snowman pajamas, knees spread apart like some stupid cowboy. It's an excited dad walk. I don't understand it, but I swear every dad I know does it. My dad did it on Christmas morning, and now so does my brother-in-law.

He parts his kids like the Red Sea and gathers me up in a hug. "You made it!"

When he pulls away, he looks beside me and, being the wonderful human he is, asks with zero disdain, "Who is this?"

"Nicholas," Nic says, extending his hand.

"Get out of town," Anne says breathless.

"Well, I just got here so..." Nic says, bashful and cute and perfect.

Brian takes his hand in a strong shake and grins.

"Cool beard, man."

"Brian can't grow one," I stage-whisper.

"Don't embarrass me in front of the cool new guy," Brian says back.

"Alright, well, uh, presents then?" Anne asks, stretching out her arms to pat the backs of her kids, who are already bolting down the hall into the next room with the Christmas tree and likely too many gifts. "I figure we'll open presents then head to Momma's, huh?" Anne asks. "If that's okay."

"It's perfect," I say.

I grab her and finally tug her close, the last but most important of the hugs.

"I'm happy you're here," she says. "And don't think we forgot about these either, Beem."

"Forgot about what?" I ask.

But, geez, I already know.

Brian is running back up the steps, and seconds later a wrapped square flies over the banister and lands on the ground in front of me. It's a matching pair of teal snowman pajamas, secured with a silver ribbon.

"And, lucky for you, I've gained weight this year," Brian yells, throwing another, bigger pair of navy-blue ones. "Get dressed too, Nicholas!"

Nic looks down at it, scans the fabric, the design, the whole kit and caboodle.

It's a lot. I know it is.

"You don't have to," I whisper to him.

But Nic simply shakes his head, and that bit of sparkle in his eye seems more watery than before.

"I'd love to," he says, bending down to pick it up and press it against his chest like it's some wonderful gift he's always wanted. Maybe it is in some weird way. And when he smiles that beautiful, dimpled grin of his, I realize maybe he's my wonderful gift. The one I didn't want but was secretly looking for the whole time.

Anne sighs, holding up her hand and gesturing in a circle around her head as if corralling a team.

"Alright, cinnamon rolls in five!"

There's a cacophony of yelling, and I'm not sure who is louder: the kids or Brian and Nicholas.

———

Christmas at Momma's care facility is the same every year, but that's not necessarily a bad thing. The staff makes it as comforting as possible with lots of Christmas lights, stockings hung on the warm fireplace, and only the best of the holiday classics playing low over the speakers. It's a perfect comfort for families on Christmas.

The kids are excited as always to see their grandma, whereas I'm nervous. Nic's hand is in mine the entire time. I can feel every warm stroke of his fingers followed by every ounce of comfort he imbues me with.

Momma is in her usual comfy chair by the fireplace. It's massive and would normally swallow her whole, but the kids fill the remaining space, crawling over her and showing off the new toys they unwrapped just this morning.

She seems interested, like maybe it does mean something to her that Buzz and Woody are gallivanting around having adventures. Even if she doesn't know who the characters are, I feel like she never forgets the kids. It's like they're engrained in her mind, a shining beacon of hope for the future to replace all she's lost along the way.

I'm awkward as I approach her. I know I am. I always am these past few years, but it's weirder this time because I'm introducing Nic. My Nic.

"Momma, this is…my…boyfriend?"

I try not to have it come out as a question, but my puppy-like head tilt definitely gives it away.

"Boyfriend," Nic echoes, giving one a dimpled smile and holding out a hand for my mom to shake.

She makes eyes at him before throwing a knowing wink at me, and I feel more at ease.

"Pleasure to meet you, Nic," she says. Elegant. Lovely. Very much like Momma.

And then we wait. Well, I wait, I guess.

I await the dreaded line of 'Where's your dad?' for the rest of the afternoon. It comes every year and, according to Anne, has been more frequent than usual lately, so I wait for it. I wait for the snow cloud looming over us waiting to break open with the rains of misplaced nostalgia.

But by midafternoon, even after we've had too many slices of honey-baked ham, eaten too many mouthfuls of warm croissants, and reluctantly swallowed down fruit cake, I have yet to hear it. There's only Momma's stray smiles and quiet sips of peppermint tea. We gift presents— framed family pictures she coos at with joy and even my gift of the latest CD Christmas album, which grants me another knowing wink.

It feels…like old Mom. Different.

When I finally get the courage to sit next to her for more than five minutes, her eyes drift down to my wrist.

"That's a beautiful watch," she says. "Looks like Frederick's."

It's time. I know it is. I await the question, the one that pulls at my chest, the one even Nic's tight handholding can't prepare me for. I'm ready. It won't hurt this year.

But nothing comes. She just smiles, like maybe she's waiting for me to say something in response. So I do.

"Yes," I say. "It was Daddy's watch."

"That's right," she responds with a nod. "You know, I miss him very much."

My throat catches. Even though the kids are zooming across the room, chasing their toys around, Brian fallen to the floor to let them use him as a makeshift set piece, Anne's head cranes toward us in surprise, and she smiles.

"Us too, Momma," she says.

I place a hand over Momma's. The jingle bells ring in the background, the hum of the music dances through our ears, and Nic places a small kiss right on the top of my forehead as he likes to do.

It's a holiday miracle, if I could believe in those.

Though, with my family and my perfect Santa—no, my perfect man—beside me, maybe I do for once.

epilogue

FOUR YEARS LATER, CHRISTMAS DAY

Nicholas

Christmas Day is always chaos. It shouldn't be, given how practiced we've gotten at booking flights out of St. Rudolph early and making sure Christmas outfits are set aside, but you try having a two-year-old who learned how to waddle-run this year.

I chase my son into my sister-in-law's living room, gathering him up in my arms and blowing a raspberry against his tummy. It's the only thing that will send him into a fit of laughter long enough to get a coat on him, a magic trick I learned a couple months ago that amazed my wife.

"Arms up," I say.

"No." He loves that word.

"Yes," I argue back.

He practically cackles, letting the coat slide on in one smooth motion.

Brian's head pokes in through the open door to the garage.

"Hey, we're gonna meet you there, okay?" he says.

Of course they got their car packed faster than us. He and Anne are like machines with their three kids.

"I'll lock up behind us!" I call.

He nods, throwing a thumbs-up before their mini-van rumbles down the road.

I open our own car door and lift my son up to the car seat in the back of our SUV. I buckle him in.

"Cinnamon rolls?" he asks.

Little dude doesn't know more than fifty words, but of course he can form that sentence, even if it does sound more like 'cim-mim rolls.'

"Nope, can't have more until we get back," I say.

"Please?"

I look both ways then nod.

"Okay, I'll sneak you half of one since it's Christmas, but don't tell Mom."

He seems pleased enough.

"Alright," I say, looping his arm in. "Last one."

"Is Grandma there?"

I pause.

It's sad, partly, because we all know it's getting close for her. Her mind isn't there much anymore. But despite that, I can't help but get choked up by my son's lingering hope. I love that about him. He's got his momma in him in that regard; they have that same optimism when it comes to Christmas.

"Yes," I say, snapping the last buckle of his car seat into place. "Grandma will be there."

He smiles and I kiss his forehead, ruffling the wild tuft of his ginger hair before making my way back into the house.

"Beem, how's it going?" I call out.

Birdie Mae comes barreling down the stairwell at my voice.

Any other day, she might have pieces of her hair askew, most of it knotted up in a bun, and be wearing some sweatshirt. Not today. Today her hair is curled, so neatly it might be easy to trail my fingers through each individual ringlet. She's in a typical tacky holiday sweater with five different Santas holding hands like those paper dolls strung up on fireplaces, tucked into a skirt with black stockings that accentuate how slender and lovely her legs are.

It takes everything I have to not kiss off the deep plum red of her lipstick, so instead I gather her in my arms and kiss her collarbone. She melts into me, and the sentiment is mutual. It's her scent, the cherry-apple combination that drives me wild.

"Get everything settled?" I ask.

She giggles into my chest and whispers, "Yeah, he says Comet is fed and happy, but I have other concerns."

I bark out a laugh. "Ten bucks we find another whoopee cushion…"

We have Cooper watching our dog, Comet, back in St. Rudolph. We were both convinced that, with the house keys, he would host some tween holiday rager on Christmas Eve, but there were no frantic calls from police last night, thank God. Though, I almost guarantee a prank or two will remain, because it's Cooper and he does Cooper things.

Birdie Mae pulls away, glancing at my getup. I'm wearing a big red coat. Not exactly lined with white fur or belted at the waist, but it's still red, and she gets this look sometimes when she sees me dressed up.

She sighs with a smile and shakes her head.

"You really should have won this year," she says.

"You're biased."

She throws her hands in the air with a grin. "I have eyes!"

"Nah, I haven't gotten that dad bod yet. But just you wait!" I pat my nonexistent belly, and she laughs, giving it a loving playful pat too.

Every year we now host a Santa competition in St. Rudolph's Square. I competed for the first time this year as opposed to strictly volunteering. I won "Most Eligible Santa" even though I'm happily head-over-snow-boots married, and ultimately Tim took home the grand prize for Santa Lookalike. He's got that old-man-looking smile that endears the soul. All I've got is a cute ass—Birdie Mae's words; not mine.

"Okay, where's Freddy?" she asks.

"In the trunk."

"Nic…"

I laugh. "Buckled and ready to go."

"And you?" she asks.

"With you, Mrs. Ryan, so I'm good to go."

She smiles, settling into my arms more.

I like that she seems relaxed. Birdie Mae is always a tornado on Christmas Day. I know it's the lingering fear of her mom's memory, something she won't ever be able to shake. And to be honest, I don't think this'll be a year where her mom remembers much, but that's okay, and she knows it's okay. It's just a part of life.

"And did you get everything you asked for?" she asks me.

She's referring to my stocking over the fireplace, which I opened this morning—right in line with Brian and Anne's—where she snuck in my favorite peppermint chocolate along with some custom guitar picks.

But I got everything I truly wanted four years ago.

I couldn't have known I would see that little girl again, the one who snuck that letter into Santa's pocket. I couldn't have known the girl who was teeming with the spirit of

Christmas would walk into St. Rudolph's local bar twenty years later as a beautiful woman to change my life. I couldn't have known she would be the angel to rescue me again, just as she had rescued me almost twenty years before.

I was a mess of a kid with my furrowed brow and teenage over-confidence. And there she was, a girl who loved her family and Christmas. She cared so much, and it settled deep in me. Something changed that day. So I uprooted my life, moved far away, and married someone who ultimately broke my heart.

And then, like magic, Birdie Mae showed up again.

Maybe I was waiting for her this whole time. To save me. To share her family. To show me what love really is.

So I simply say, "Yes. Everything I've ever wanted."

And I think she knows what I truly mean because, despite the lipstick, she leans in and plants a big ol' kiss on my lips. The color probably bleeds onto my gray beard, but I don't care.

"Merry Christmas, Nicholas," she whispers against my mouth.

"Merry Christmas, Birdie Mae."

THE END

thanks, etc.

This book is my love letter to Christmas. Growing up in the 1990s and early 2000s, December was like my family's holy grail of holiday months. We made sugar cookies, decorated our tree with too many ornaments that literally sent the tree falling down, and watched all the old cartoons like Rudolph and Santa Claus Is Coming to Town. Even as I'm nearing 30, I still get excited around this time, so I knew I had to bind all those special feelings into a book.

I wasn't sure who would like this premise. Some woman who just couldn't seem to date anyone except Santa? Weird. But, the more I thought about it, I realized this train wasn't stopping, and I'm so happy I continued. Thank you, the reader, first and foremost for giving this weird book a chance! I hope you enjoyed reading it as much as I loved writing it.

Thank you to my Mom, Dad, and my brother for making holidays memorable. I can still feel the sting of cold Christmas mornings. Ah, good times.

To my editor, Caitlin, for making this book readable. You're a wizard. I always get a weird sense of both anxiety and satisfaction when your notes land in my inbox, and I wouldn't want it any other way.

To my sister-in-law for always listening to me when I rant about books. I mean, literally, every time. I don't know how you do it. I also don't know how my brother happened to marry the person who would eventually become my best friend. Maybe he has a sense for those kinds of things.

To Jenny Bunting for being my author soul sister and letting me know when something is a good idea or if I'm just being neurotic. Sometimes it's both.

To Allie G. who always gets me more hyped about my books than I already am. If you don't have a friend suggesting you write fanfiction for your own books--and having you seriously consider it--then you need to get one. But you can't have my Allie.

To my beta readers, some of whom decided it would be fun to pick completely anonymous joke names which I love: "Santa's Favorite Elf," "The One and Only True Love of My Life Who Isn't My Husband," Emily Lierrman, Carrie Driscoll, Elizabeth Anderson, Jenny Bailey, Jen Morris, and Kolin. Thank you, thank you, thank you for being the first to read this book that hadn't been, and maybe shouldn't have been, seen by anyone. You guys will be happy to know that I toned down the Santa kink by a lot so thank you. Birdie Mae thanks you as well.

And, finally, to the love of my life: my husband. Thank you for supporting, and actively encouraging, my hectic schedule as I achieve this crazy author dream. Thanks for inspiring all my older, swoony heroes with your hilarious one-liners and Mr. Fantastic hair. I promise I don't have a Santa kink, but honestly who would know except us, anyway?

about the author

Julie Olivia writes spicy romantic comedies and, after writing this one, now wishes she could only set them during the holiday season. During her free time, she likes driving around to look at Christmas lights, eating way too many peppermint-flavored chocolates, and swooning over Jude Law and Jack Black in the movie, The Holiday. Julie lives in Atlanta, Georgia with her husband who enjoys socks as Christmas presents and their cat who just wishes all the jingle bells would stop.

Sign-up for the newsletter for book updates, special offers, and VIP exclusives!: julieoliviaauthor.com/newsletter

facebook.com/julieoliviaauthor
instagram.com/julieoliviaauthor
amazon.com/author/julieoliviaauthor
bookbub.com/authors/julie-olivia

Printed in Great Britain
by Amazon